# Jesse Jameson

## and the (2300)
## Curse of Caldazar

*Sean Wright — 22-5-04*

### Sean Wright

*A Crowswing Book*

LET THE JOURNEY BEGIN ...

By Sean Wright and available from Crowswing Books

# Jesse Jameson Series

Otherwise known as the Jesse Jameson Alpha to Omega Series

The Golden Glow (Book 1) (2003)

The Bogie Beast (Book 2) (2003)

The Curse of Caldazar (Book 3) (2004)

The Vampire Vault (Book 4) (2004)

The Stonehenge of Spelfindial (Book 5) (2005)

The Earthwitch of Evenstorm (Book 6) (2005)


*Other fiction:*

The Twisted Root of Jaarfindor (2004)

Dark Tales of Time and Space (2005)

*This is the third book in the*
*Jesse Jameson Alpha to Omega Series written*
*by Sean Wright and the author dedicates it to*
*Linda, Keith, Karen, and Susie.*

First published in hardback in 2004 by Crowswing Books.

10 9 8 7 6 5 4 3 2 1

**www.crowswingbooks.co.uk**

(Special Limited Edition 2500)

A CIP catalogue record for this book is available from the British Library.

ISBN 0-9544374-3-8

# CONTENTS

The white lie like the dark truth can often save a life ... however, truth is in the mind of the Seer, and belief is for those who do not know.

## Praise for Sean Wright

'An amazing collection and one which will surely rival any other for sheer number of books alone. Fabulous. A collector's dream.' *Nigel Eastman, sqwubbsybooks.co.uk*

'I really enjoyed the Golden Glow (Book 1 in the series). A brilliant debut novel which is fast becoming a modern day classic.' *Alison Cresswell, co-producer of the JK Rowling BBC Omnibus documentary*

'I have read and enjoyed Jesse Jameson and the Golden Glow and can see why you have so many fans ...' *Caradoc King, literary agent to Philip Pullman*

'The latest star in a golden age of fantasy books for children.' *Eastern Daily Press*

'Highly recommended. A very good read.' *GP Taylor, bestselling children's author*

'Great plot ... weird characters.' *CBBC Book Review section*

'Super and ideal for all ages.' *Shadow-mania.com*

One

# The Hiding Place

The High Witch, Zundrith, clung to the shadows of the twilight, muttering spells and casting curses into the towering waterfall. As each splash of freezing water fell, it instantly turned into another jagged tooth of ice. The riverbed was a mountainous mass of sparkling teeth that stretched high into the clouds, formed over centuries, ever increasing, and never melting. Though she wished more than anything to move - just one step - she was welded to the river bank. However, she knew who had tricked her, who had enslaved her for almost a thousand years. It would not be long before she would be free, and then there would be mayhem and oceans of blood.

'One day soon, my pathetic little retinue,' Zundrith hissed. 'I shall climb this mountain of ice and teeth and blood and bones. I shall conquer this blasted summit, and free you all. Then we will crush our enemies and all who stand in our way. But not before I have my revenge for the sisters held in that glass prison!'

In the palm of her open hand, a tiny red flame flickered. She whispered to the flame fondly, in a language so harsh and fetid that to ears other than the darkest of witches its tones hurt like fists punching and pounding. She curled her upper lip into a grimace of pleasure, and sucked the heat from the flame. She watched through squinting black eyes as the thin ribbon of blue smoke snaked into the icy air. She hissed and it turned into a corkscrew of rhino horn, and then exploded into a million tiny fragments of dust. Crushed - as her enemies would be - she studied the gently drifting particles.

Her contorted skeleton-thin body shuddered and she howled demonically, calling others from the icy wastelands of the Monstrous Mountains. Many thousands of many millions came swiftly and obediently. Dark things floated in and out of focus, huddled around the dirty folds of her long black cloak, basking in the unnatural nightfall that surrounded her.

'Go, my pretties,' Zundrith whispered coldly. 'Go now and bring the child, Jesse, to me.'

As the hoardes of blurred demons did her bidding, her vile brother, Dumdrith, became visible from the shadows beside her, wet and dripping purple goo. He was her closest blood-relative, and she hated him totally.

With lightning speed he jerked his neck.

Cracking bone and sinew at the base of his skull, a mouth, with rotten gnashing incisors, opened between a mass of tangled red hair. A swollen black tongue slipped out, and a dazed frog appeared. It plopped into his hairy wart-ridden hand like sticky jam from a pot.

Pretending pleasure, Zundrith quizzed, 'For me brother dear?'

Dumdrith nodded stupidly, unable to speak since his sister had moved his mouth to the back of his head and frozen his tongue. He offered the frog to her, afraid to look anywhere but her protruding webbed feet.

Zundrith cackled as she squeezed the fat green frog in her fingers until its eyes almost popped out of its head. She opened her jaws wide and flashed silver razor teeth.

'What else have you stored in your head, brother? I'm starving! Feed me now!'

*

Jesse was the last to step out of the Spiral Gate. Three crescent moons shone a silvery light throughout the forest. A slender band of mist clung to skeletal trees. The air was humid and oppressive. In the far distance thunder cracked and blue lightning flashed, electrifying the inky night sky.

'Where are we?' Jesse asked.

'Caldazar,' Zarlan-Jagr said, leading them along a narrow, winding tree-lined track.

'Impossible,' the Dragon Hunter said. He was armour-plated from head to toe in a bronze-coloured metal. His shield was decorated with the symbol of a two-headed, bronze axe, its shaft entwined with a black snake. 'Caldazar is a myth.'

'Yes, it is a myth,' Zarlan-Jagr replied, nodding. 'A living myth.'

'If what you claim is true, wizard,' the Dragon Hunter scoffed, 'then we have travelled back in time to the Unknown Kingdoms of Ancient Times. How can this be?'

'Caldazar is an ancient city, but the stories about its destruction thousands of years ago were deliberately exaggerated.'

'Why?' Jake asked. He brushed his mousy brown hair out of his eyes, and blinked nervously behind his glasses.

'I would have thought that was obvious,' the wizard said, stopping at the edge of the forest. 'Look for yourself. Have you ever seen a sight so magnificent?'

Ahead of them Caldazar rose like dark icebergs out of a sea of mountains. Within its towering fortification of jagged rock, thousands of narrow black monoliths and bastions pressed against the sky. The windows were thin zig-zagged slits, seemingly slashed by monstrous claws. The black marble from which it was built glimmered like blurred starlight beneath a rushing stream. Two slender, twisted spires stood taller than all the rest, as if immense skewers penetrating the sky. At their tips were spinning discs. Jesse could see that they were greedily sucking in the light of the three moons. Every shape was harsh, jarring and repulsive.

The companions stood there on the edge of the forest speechless for a full five minutes. The sheer vastness of Caldazar was impossible to grasp. Jesse kept blinking her eyes, closing them, reopening them, sure that the awesome vision would vanish like a mirage. But it did not. If anything, its total domination of the landscape grew.

'I have never seen such a sight,' the Dragon Hunter admitted.

'Tis a wondrous monster of a place,' Iggywig added. 'Be the rest of the monster-myth a-true, too?'

Zarlan-Jagr did not answer.

'We must hurry,' the wizard said, leading them down a hillside track which would eventually bring them to the River Stark. 'It is too dangerous to remain out in the open.'

'Why?' Jesse wanted to know.

Again, the wizard would not be drawn into conversation.

'Let us fly,' he said, and using their own wings, Zarlan-Jagr and Iggywig flew off into the mist.

Jesse transformed into a dragon, and the Hunter and Jake rode on her back. They didn't speak as they soared down the hillside and up the valley. Jesse thought that it was odd that they kept to the track, winding like a great snake, when they could have made better time flying in a straight line above the treetops.

Half an hour later, Zarlan-Jagr flew up a slope, hardly slowing his speed. Suddenly, before them

Jesse and the Dragon Hunter saw a wide clearing. Two enormous, ancient trees rose like living sentinels out of the undergrowth.

'The Portal of Talonscar,' the wizard whispered. He landed on the soft earth and turned to his companions.

'What is the Portal of Talonscar?' Jesse asked.

'A bridge between one dimension and another dimension.'

'All I see are two very old trees,' Jesse said.

'In the Kingdom of Caldazar, all maybe not quite as it appears.' He wriggled the fingers of his ringless hand. A small obsidian stone glittered in his palm. 'Take it and place it in the middle of your forehead. Make sure you close your eyes.'

Jesse took the obsidian and pressed it against her forehead. She closed her eyes. Immediately, she felt giddy, a tingling sensation where the obsidian was resting. Then, a whoosh of bright blue light entered her mind, and she could see them all around her even though her eyes were tightly shut - Iggywig, Jake, the Dragon Hunter, and Zarlan-Jagr. Beyond them, and in between the two trees, she saw a mass of swirling light and energy. It was shaped like a large, round spinning door.

'I see it,' she whispered. 'It's some kind of doorway.'

'The Portal of Talonscar,' the wizard said. He uttered a few foreign words and an arch of yellow light engulfed them to make a shelter. 'Fear not – this arch will keep our words private. You may keep the Seeing-Stone. It will prove more than useful in the future. It holds great magic - gifted from the Elders of Elriad. My mentor gave it to me many years ago when I was a young mage and my path before me lay unseen and troubled. Now I pass on its secrets to you, Jesse Jameson. There's more magic inside it than a young fairy could ever need. But you will come face to face with more danger than a fairy child should ever endure.' The wizard's face darkened. 'But a word of warning - use the Seeing-Stone wisely and only when no other course of action can be taken. It is not a toy but a tool of immense power. With it comes responsibility, to yourself and others. Do not tip the Great Unbalancing in the favour of the Darkness. Seek its counsel and its advice, for it will guide you along many Paths of Illumination.'

'Thank you,' Jesse said, and she watched as the arch of light dissolved. She slipped the obsidian into her pocket. She had many questions bursting inside. She wanted to know what kind of magic the obsidian held and who were the Elders of Elriad, but her thoughts were whisked away.

'The guardians of this sacred place have arrived. Say and do nothing,' Zarlan said. 'Whatever happens. Is that clear?'

'Yes,' Jesse said, 'but-'

'Please, do not ask me another question,' Zarlan-Jagr cut in calmly. 'Many living and non-living things work for the Rulers of Caldazar. Rocks, trees, birds, even the very air we breathe - many things here are like eyes and ears to the Rulers. It is difficult to tell the true from the false.

Even as I speak, there is a good chance that what we say will be heard and passed on to the Clerics of Information.' He narrowed his eyes, deep in thought. 'I have said more than enough. We are being watched and listened to. Now remember-'

'Do and say nothing, whatever happens,' Jesse interrupted. 'Yes, I think we understand.'

'Good,' the wizard said. 'You may prefer to close your eyes when the Wild Winds of Murokchi come. And, Dragon Hunter, do not unleash your sword. If you do, you'll be struck down dead where you stand by the spirit that guards this sacred place.'

'What is the name of this guardian?' the Dragon Hunter asked tersely.

'Her name is Masdemdresa.'

'I know of her from childhood stories. How can she be real? She is a mythical being.'

'She is real, my friend. She can and will cross the threshold of many dimensions in pursuit of her enemy. Do not offend Masdemdresa. Is that clear?'

The Dragon Hunter nodded and instinctively gripped the hilt of his sword in readiness. Jesse gave him an icy glare. He withdrew his hand, his fingers twitching anxiously.

They did not have to wait long. The Wild Winds of Murokchi shook the leaves from the trees, and bent them violently to and fro. Jesse closed her eyes and covered her face. Dust and grit and forest debris blasted her. She leaned hard into the wind, afraid that she would be blown over.

The Wild Winds of Murokchi penetrated her

mind, probing for secrets and betrayals and treacherous thoughts. For ten minutes, a hurricane expanded and swirled in her head. She laughed and screamed and cursed and cried as the Wild Winds tore at her memories, dragging them to the surface. Overwhelmed, she sank to her knees.

A woman's soothing voice spoke to her in a language she did not understand. A beautiful face appeared, with wide dark eyes and silky flaxen hair, untouched by the Wild Winds. She had long delicate fangs either side of her mouth. She was a vampire spirit. Her presence made Jesse feel extraordinarily calm.

'Masdemdresa,' the woman whispered, and the sound of the words broke into pieces and circled in Jesse's mind like a mantra.

'Masdemdresa,' Jesse echoed.

Then, in an instant, the Wild Winds of Murokchi left her, sucking out all the negative thoughts locked in the secret chambers of her mind. Jake collapsed on the earth, holding his head. The Dragon Hunter had been forced to his hands and knees. Iggywig was rolling drunkenly through mounds of dried leaves, giggling, jabbering like a baby.

'We have been cleansed, good guardian. Thank you. May we enter?' Zarlan-Jagr asked, approaching the Portal of Talonscar with his head bowed in respect.

'You and the one called Jesse may enter,' Masdemdresa's voice answered. There was no visible sign of her, except a small ball of purple light that hovered a metre above the undergrowth. The rest must wait in the clearing until your return. I will protect them from the Caldazarian soldiers if they are foolish enough to attack.'

'As you wish,' Zarlan-Jagr said, bowing with reverence. He conjured a small silver bangle from the air and offered it to her as a gift.

Jesse shot the Dragon Hunter a wary glance, anticipating his protest. He issued none. He still seemed shocked to discover that a mythical vampire-character from his own childhood wasn't fiction at all.

'Take my sword of light,' the Dragon Hunter said.

'It's all right,' Zarlan-Jagr said. 'We won't need it.'

'I did not mean my sword for you,' the Dragon Hunter said curtly. 'It's for Jesse's protection.'

'She will not need it. I am all the protection she needs, and she has the great magic of the Seeing-Stone. Besides, the creatures of Talonscar are our friends and allies. The Union of Thirteen fought side by side with them during the Sixth Caldazarian War. We are amongst friends here.'

'That maybe so,' the Dragon Hunter said. 'But I am Jesse's guardian. If I cannot enter the Portal of Talonscar, then my sword must. We are in the Unknown Kingdoms. There is much danger here.'

'There is more danger here, you are right. But there is no danger in Talonscar. It is a safe haven.'

He wriggled his fingers and on his open palm appeared a small glass egg. Jesse squinted and peered inside it. What she saw astonished her.

'The witches!' she yelled. 'You have them trapped inside!'

'I believe Dendrith may be able to help us with a counter-charm. So I took the liberty of bringing her and her sister with us.'

'I have a better way to get the witches' help,' the Dragon Hunter said, taking the glass egg from the wizard. He shook it violently, like an angry child shaking a paperweight filled with watery snow. 'Tell us the counter-charm, or I will shake the life out of you!'

'They are already dead,' Jesse said, opening her hand. 'And I don't think brute force will get them to talk.'

'You have a better idea?'

'No,' she said lamely. 'But I'm not comfortable with torture.'

'You give them too much respect. They have caused us all so much suffering. Now we have the advantage. We should use it.'

'Maybe, but not like that,' she said, extending her hand further.

Reluctantly, the Dragon Hunter stopped shaking the egg and tossed it into her palm.

'Thank you.'

The Dragon Hunter shrugged, and turned away.

Jesse opened her mouth to offer words of comfort, but thought better of it. His concern for Perigold was plain to see. They all missed the soothsayer badly.

Jesse gazed into the glass egg. The essence of the witches was still swirling around inside like two mini tornadoes. Their life-force was dark and disturbed, streaked with green and red strands of smoke.

'Free us, and we will spare your life, child,' Dendrith's voice echoed in Jesse's head. 'Smash the egg! You know you want to. You know it is the right thing to do!'

'Yes, do as my sister says, child,' Gwendrith added. 'Release us and we will give you the counter-charm to release your precious grandfather.'

Jesse felt an unstoppable urge to smash the egg. She scanned the undergrowth for a rock. Her mind felt as if a clamp had been tightened, squeezing all thoughts from it but one: smash the egg!

'Yes, that's right, my pretty,' Dendrith said. 'You must do it. Now!'

'Thank you,' the wizard said, snatching the egg from Jesse's grasp. 'Let me keep this safe. We don't want an accident, now do we?'

As if being sucked down a plug hole, Jesse's mind returned to her in a flash of dizziness and light. She clasped her pounding head, and stumbled. Iggywig steadied her.

'There will be other times,' she heard Dendrith saying vaguely in her mind. 'You will help us, we know. You are made from the same stuff. We are all women - slaves in a world of men. Sisters always unite together eventually.'

'Get her out of my head!' Jesse yelled. 'I can't think straight.'

Zarlan-Jagr brushed her forehead with his fingertips and the witch's dark magic vanished. She sat down heavily on a rock, not saying anything for a few minutes. The Dragon Hunter and Iggywig comforted her as best they could, but all she could think about was the witches' smallness and vast power. It seemed unbelievable that creatures so tiny and helpless, could command such influence and strength.

'How did you shrink them?' she asked eventually.

Zarlan wriggled his finger tips. 'Magic,' he said, winking. 'Some kind of a deal may be struck to awaken Perigold. That is why I have brought them along.'

'Perigold?' Jesse said. She felt a surge of excitement.

The wizard raised his eyebrows.

'He's here?' she said.

Zarlan-Jagr nodded.

'I will see, Perigold,' the Dragon Hunter said, his golden eyes narrowing to slits. Swiftly, he slid his sword from its scabbard and held it to the wizard's throat. 'And you will take me to him.'

'What are you doing?' Jesse shouted. 'Put your sword away!'

'It's all right,' Zarlan said calmly to Jesse. He looked at the Dragon Hunter without fear in his eyes. 'It would give me great pleasure to reunite you with your old friend. If it were up to me, then we would all walk through the Portal. But Masdemdresa has already decided who will and who will not enter Talonscar. It is out of my hands.'

'Then you will enter alone, and bring Perigold to us.'

Zarlan ignored the Dragon Hunter's request.

'The Union of the Thirteen has sworn to protect Perigold in this time of conflict and trouble. We make decisions together, because those decisions affect us all. So you see the impossible position I am in?'

'I will protect Perigold,' the Dragon Hunter repeated. 'If you truly are a white wizard, you will help us, not hinder us.'

'As I have already said, the Thirteen has sworn to protect him.' He looked down at the tiny witches trapped inside the glass egg. 'And until a counter-charm can be activated, that is what we will do.'

'What gives you the right to name yourselves protectors of Perigold?'

'Please put down the sword,' Jesse said, but they both seemed not to notice her or the sword.

'It is too delicate a matter to explain here.' Zarlan-Jagr motioned with his free hand at the trees and rocks around them. 'I think you know what I mean?'

'Why are you so interested in protecting Perigold?' Jake asked nervously. 'W-what is he to you?'

'Be a-good questioning,' Iggywig said, now recovered from his giggling fit.

'I cannot answer those questions,' Zarlan-Jagr

said.

'Cannot, or will not?' the Dragon Hunter challenged.

'Listen, please, to reason. I understand your concerns, but Perigold has no finer protectors. As his friends, you are also under the protection of the Thirteen.'

'Maybe you are not Perigold's or our protectors,' the Dragon Hunter said, moving the sword closer to the wizard's throat. 'Maybe you are our captors?'

'If that were true, you would not be free to leave, as you are right now. If it were true, I would not have helped you defeat Dendrith. And I and the Thirteen would not be risking our lives to help you find a counter-charm.'

'B-b-but you said, back on Island Gloom, you'd take us to Perigold,' Jake said anxiously. 'N-now you are saying it's not possible.'

'For Jesse it is possible. Masdemdresa has granted her entry to Talonscar. Let's go now.'

Jesse had an anxious look in her blue eyes. What Jake had said made sense. Yet on the other hand, Zarlan's words rang true, too.

She glanced uncertainly at the witches in the egg. She could feel their hatred like a hand around her throat. Despite their imprisonment, she felt that their powers as ghost-witches were formidable.

'I don't think I should go without my friends,' Jesse said at last.

'Every moment spent in the shadow of Caldazar is a moment gained by the Caldazarian soldiers, who will be making their way to this place as we speak. We will be surrounded with no route of escape. We must hurry.'

'Then we shall die fighting,' the Dragon Hunter said proudly, 'while you hide like a rat in Talonscar.'

'Please, my friends, enough of this.' Zarlan-Jagr's voice softened. 'We have said too much already. The Rulers of Caldazar will be informed. So we must hurry. Once inside Talonscar, we can talk freely.'

'Be my humble opinionings,' Iggywig said, 'that we must be a-trusting good Zarlan. Tis a wizard of much goodings. He be a legend to my people. My support he be a-having.'

'Does he really?' Jesse asked.

Iggywig smiled broadly. 'Zarlan be a-good wizard.'

The Dragon Hunter nodded thoughtfully. His respect for Iggywig was clear to see. His face relaxed a little. 'But I still have concerns about us being here, left in such a vulnerable position. I do not like being kept in the dark.'

'I am sorry to sound so vague,' Zarlan said. 'All that I know, I will tell. But not here.'

'Then hurry as quickly as you can,' the Dragon Hunter said, 'so that we can leave this place and return to Troth with Perigold, cured of this cowardly charm.'

'What about the soldiers?' Jake said, trembling. He gazed around. The undergrowth was dense and dark, alive with the creatures of the night.

'We will hurry as quickly as we can,' Zarlan-Jagr said. He patted Jake's back.

'Until your return, then,' the Dragon Hunter said, sitting down heavily on a small boulder.

Jesse hugged her friends and strode through the Portal with the wizard. They did not look back.

Two

# Talonscar

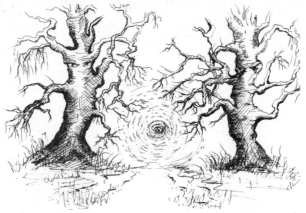

Zundrith spat at the cascading water and pushed her brother to the ground without moving a muscle. Her mind was a powerful weapon. He fell awkwardly, cracking his head on the iron hard ice.

'Get up, you pathetic creature,' she growled. She wanted to tear her eyes away from the visions she could see in the waterfall, but she was enthralled by Jesse Jameson's struggle with Dendrith's and Gwendrith's magic.

'Help is on its way, Sisters in Suffering,' she said to the images appearing from the waterfall. 'Though you do not know it, my hordes will help you escape to *me*. You shall have your precious golden glow and I the Seeing-Stone and my first steps to freedom and revenge. Soon, we shall meet, Sisters in Suffering.'

She turned her torso slowly to gaze down on her brother. She opened her mouth like a ravenous ugly chick.

'Feed me now,' she demanded, and Dumdrith obeyed her without question.

*

Jesse whooshed at a fantastic speed through a swirling tunnel of light and dark. It was like being dragged backwards by giant hands. She felt dizzy and sick. Then it was over. She exploded out of the tunnel, breaking the golden surface of a heavy warm liquid. She bobbed up and down for a few moments, gathering her bearings. Looking around, she could see that she was floating in a pool, inside a large cavern. Gathered all around, hovering a few inches above a narrow ledge, she saw dozens of transparent, golden beings.

'Greetings from the Inner Kingdom of Talonscar,' one of them said softly. 'My name is Trelakum. Take my hand, please. I will lead you to Perigold.'

The Talonscarian people were three feet tall, with large black oval eyes that dominated otherwise featureless faces. They had a single small hole where a nose might have been, and thin slits for mouths. Their arms were long and spindly. They did not walk on floppy legs, but floated inches above the ground.

Trelakum helped them out of the pool. Jesse was surprised at Trelakum's great strength, for he scarcely seemed to use any force at all. She found it difficult not to keep staring at the contents of Trelakum's body. She could see his three hearts beating slowly; his transparent ribcage rising and falling; his lungs inhaling and exhaling; the juices of his last meal in the process of digestion. Jake would have thought it absolutely fantastic, Jesse knew. He loved the macabre. He would be terribly jealous when she told him about the Talonscarian people.

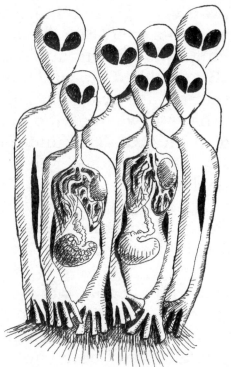

They travelled through a vast network of chambers and caverns, along narrow winding tunnels, and up steep stone steps. At last, some twenty exhausting minutes later, Trelakum halted outside an arched doorway. The door looked heavy. Some kind of metal, perhaps?

'Clathdor!' Trelakum spat.

The door shot upwards into the lintel above, making a loud swishing sound. Trelakum ushered them inside, and spat another word which Jesse didn't quite catch. The door whooshed shut.

Jesse gazed around the dome-shaped room. It was dimly lit with a green light, the source of which she could not locate. In a circle, around the outside of the room, she counted thirteen rectangular slabs. Lying motionless on eight of them, she saw a host of creatures. She recognised Perigold at once, and ran quickly to him.

'It's Jesse,' she whispered, holding his limp hand.

Perigold did not respond.

Jesse winced, horrified. She could now see Perigold's face. It was covered in a fine web-like material. Crawling on the mass of web, busy spinning more fine thread, were hundreds of tiny spiders. No, not spiders! These creatures had hundreds of legs – a sort of centipede-spider. A centi-spider?

'How long has he been like this?' Jesse asked Trelakum.

'He's been here just over a day.'

'The webbing?'

'It only began a few hours ago. We think it is part of Dendrith's original charm.'

'Haven't you tried to … kill the things?'

'We have tried, but more creatures simply reappear.'

'What about the web? It looks as if it'll smother his mouth.' Jesse's eyes widened in alarm. 'He'll stop breathing!'

'That's what we thought to begin with, but

we've been monitoring Perigold's heart-rate and breathing closely. He's fine. Whatever it is the creatures are doing, it doesn't seem to be affecting Perigold's vital signs.'

'It's disgusting!' Jesse felt an uncontrollable urge to crush a creature in between her fingers. The urge overwhelmed her and she grabbed one. It made a small popping sound, and a little green blood squirted into her hand. The creature squealed and vanished. Seconds later, it reappeared in exactly the same spot she had taken it from.

'As I explained,' Trelakum said. 'These little fellows seem indestructible. Dendrith's magic is still powerful, even though she is no longer with us in the flesh.'

Zarlan-Jagr stepped forward with the glass egg in his hand.

'What are you going to do with them?' Jesse nodded at Dendrith and Gwendrith.

'I'm not sure,' he said, winking so that the witches couldn't see him. 'What do you suggest?'

'Something painful,' Jesse said, playing along.

'Yes. Something painful and slow.'

A tiny voice shouted from the egg. 'Let us out!'

'Use your magic to get yourself out,' Zarlan-Jagr teased.

Dendrith's ghostly form turned to a bright shade of emerald green and then raged blood red.

Jesse could see that her anger was boiling her.

'You know that is ... impossible.'

'Really?' Zarlan-Jagr said, faking surprise. 'Well, that puts you in a difficult position, little witch, doesn't it?'

'Do not call me little witch.'

'Why not, *little* witch? Are you going to turn me into a worm and stamp on me?'

'No, something much worse.'

'Now what could that be?'

'I don't know,' Dendrith said sarcastically. 'You're a wizard, you figure it out.'

He held the glass egg closer to his face.

'I'd love to play mind games with you, little witch, but I haven't got time. Now tell me the counter-charm to release Perigold, or-'

'Or you'll what?' Dendrith cut across him. 'Kill

me?'

'That I have already done. Stuck in that glass prison for the rest of time, now that's an idea that doesn't bear thinking about for too long.'

'You wouldn't,' Gwendrith said, her voice quivering.

'If your sister doesn't tell me the counter-charm, then she leaves me no choice.'

'You wouldn't dare,' Gwendrith said.

Zarlan-Jagr pulled a woeful face and nodded.

'He's bluffing,' Dendrith said. 'His precious Union of Thirteen wouldn't agree to such a barbaric punishment. They are good and noble – remember? They have a moral code of conduct. They would never break it.'

'Look around you,' the wizard said. 'What do you see?'

Eight of the thirteen slabs had sleeping creatures on them, some human-looking, but others elfin or goblin or troll. One was a hunky-punk, known as Tray Mondial, and the last creature unknown.

Jesse read the gold nameplates fixed to the end of each slab.

*Laike du Puttchen (Transcended)*
*May Demigould (Ascended)*
*Wrangton Jeremies (Sleeping)*
*Tray Mondial (Sleeping)*
*Geo-Staibbe (Descended)*
*Faulken Gray (Sleeping)*
*Beattie Valderville (Sleeping)*

*Trondian-Yor (Missing)*
*Xan-Ku (Sleeping)*
*Sylvan Swiftord (Sleeping)*
*Edgar van der Stargazer (Sleeping)*
*Perigold de Lacjard (Sleeping)*
*Zarlan-Jagr (Accounted)*

'Eight of the Thirteen are sleeping, as well you know. Surely you recognise some of them?' Zarlan-Jagr said. He walked over to one of the slabs, and put the egg down on a ledge above the sleeping creature's head. 'Remember him?'

'Wrangton Jeremies,' Dendrith spat. 'How could I forget that meddling miser?'

'And her?' Zarlan-Jagr said, pointing to the woman lying motionless on the next slab. 'Remember?'

'May Demigould. Pathetic white witch if ever I saw one. Useless, goody-goody. Why are they here?'

'A question I am sure you can answer more fully than I,' the wizard said. 'After all, it was your magic which rendered them into a deep sleep from which only you can wake them.'

Dendrith laughed loudly. 'Is that what you think? You're a stupid old fool. I had nothing to do with these or any of the others who sleep like helpless babies in this rotten cell. You are wasting your time with me.'

'I think not,' Zarlan-Jagr said, and he produced a black cloth from nowhere and threw it on top of the glass egg. 'Eternity in darkness is a long time, little witch.'

'You are making a mistake,' Dendrith said. 'It is not me who holds the counter-charm to release Perigold or the rest of your pathetic Thirteen.'

'You lie.'

'No. You deceive yourself. I am not powerful enough to evoke such a charm on so many.'

'Then who is?'

'I don't know his true name. Only his public name – the New Master of Darkness.'

'Liar!'

'Have it your way. I do not have what you want.'

'Then why did you transform into Perigold? You know more than you say.'

There was a stony silence, which the ghost-witch broke after a few minutes.

'He came to me in a vision in the dead of night – a few hours before the Rumble struck. He said that he had a proposition for me, a way to trick you, a way to get the fairy child's golden glow. It sounded so easy, transforming into Perigold. It *was* easy, until the high and mighty Zarlan-Jagr butted his big fat nose into my business.

'The New Master of Darkness said that he wanted Perigold de Lacjard for his own purposes. I asked no questions. It seemed the safest thing to do. I sensed he was a creature of unfathomable power and even greater malice. For my part, I got close to Jesse Jameson, and almost snatched the glow. It was a simple deal. Such a pity I failed to use my advantage. I will not be so stupid next time, my pretty. One day, I will have your golden glo-'

'An interesting story,' Zarlan-Jagr said. 'But I do not believe a word of it. You are bluffing, little witch.'

'No,' Dendrith said wearily. 'That's what happened.'

'What did he look like?' Jesse asked, trying to hide the concern in her voice at the witch's threat.

'Like all the malice and hatred in all the Kingdoms forged together into one grotesque form that even I could barely stand to look at without feeling sick from fear. It was a powerful vision.'

'I find that hard to believe,' the wizard said.

'I found it hard to accept myself. But this creature was like nothing I have encountered before. His evil intent was far greater than any of us in Finnigull or Troth have knowledge of. His very presence redefines evil and darkness. He was glorious in his foul thoughts, magnificent in his evil scheming.'

'Was he my father?' Jesse asked.

Dendrith let out a short ironic burst of laughter.

'The Bogie Beast is no match for this foul creature. I can assure you of that. Look around you – at the magnificent eight. Soon, the creature will put the remaining Union of Thirteen into deep sleeps, too. Then I and my sister will be freed, to serve him. I urge you to run and hide as best you can. The New Master is darker than the sucking black holes of space. Run and hide, while you still have a chance!'

*

Dendrith ranted on and on about the New Master of Darkness, until Jesse and Zarlan-Jagr became tired of her. If she had a counter-charm, then she had no intention of revealing it. Putting the glass egg in one of the many pockets of his long deep purple coat, the wizard wriggled his fingers and cast a Muting and Deafening Charm on the witch, which meant she could neither hear nor speak. The silence was bliss.

'What now?' Jesse asked.

'We need help in finding the New Master of Darkness,' the wizard said. 'In the depths of the Skogsra Forest there lives a legendary tracker. He may be able to assist us in our search.'

'But you told Dendrith that you didn't believe her story.'

'I know,' the wizard said, winking. 'I lied.'

Jesse eyed him suspiciously. 'Why?'

'I can't help it,' he said, grinning. 'All good wizards are trained to lie unmercilessly without shame. It's a talent you should work on, Jesse. You never know when you might need it.'

'But ... that's dishonest.'

'Exactly.'

Jesse was lost for words.

As they left the caverns of Talonscar and returned to the Dragon Hunter, Jake, and Iggywig, a plan of action had already formulated in the wizard's mind.

Jesse felt a sudden twinge of doubt about the wizard. Could he be trusted? She wasn't sure anymore.

Three

# The Skogsra Forest

Zarlan-Jagr led the way through the Skogsra Forest towards the distant sprawl of the never-ending night of Caldazar. As soon as they had sneaked inside, monumental trees enveloped them in near darkness. Myriad moonbeams cut between the covering branches, puncturing the undergrowth with a dazzling harsh silver light.

Jesse listened to the quiver of leaves in the breeze. It undulated through the forest, causing the branches to crack and squeak like ancient coffin lids slowly rising from the inside.

Jesse clung tightly to Iggywig's hand.

To begin with their progress was steady. As they probed deeper into the Skogsra Forest the trees crowded together, their lofty, deformed roots making it difficult to keep on a direct route. They blundered along as best they could.

Suddenly Zarlan-Jagr stopped.

'Blessed forest,' he cursed, untangling his coat-tails from a gnarled root and kicking a bramble away that clung to his trousers. 'It's changed its track through to Caldazar again. I hate it when it does that.'

'What do you mean - again?' Jesse enquired.

'I used to play in this forest when I was a child. It's where I learned much of the natural magic – the minor arts such as shape-shifting, word-spell illusions and the like. My mentor from Elriad sent me here to study the herbs and befriend the spirits of the forest. Being a child, I was more interested in games. One I played was against the forest itself. It was called *Tracker.*'

'What are the rules of *Tracker?*'

'There are no rules as such, just a goal: get out of the forest before the Skogsra hunts you down and devours your flesh.'

'You're kidding?' Jesse said.

Zarlan-Jagr shook his head. 'It was all part of my training to come of age as a mage.' He swept his hand all around. 'This forest is alive. Now that the creatures and spirits and trees know I'm here, they think it's time to play *Tracker* again.'

Jesse felt the obsidian in her pocket. 'Could I use the Seeing-Stone's magic in here?'

'You could, but only when there is no other course of action open, only when a life is in danger of being lost. The Seeing-Stone's magic is not a small matter. Shape-shifting and curse-casting are very minor arts in comparison. Remember: the Calm has been restored in many Kingdoms, to use the Seeing-Stone's power needlessly would tip the balance back again to the Darkness.'

Jesse looked at the wizard, dumbfounded. She had felt his words like a musician feels the drum beat – pulsing deep in her heart, deep in her soul. She looked at the Dragon Hunter for reassurance. He simply shrugged, fingers twitching on the hilt of his sword.

'If we get separated,' Zarlan-Jagr said, 'I will wait for you at the Trading Post on the outskirts of Caldazar. And remember, the Skogsra will pretend to be your friends, your guides, your helpers in an effort to lure you to their burrows. They are powerless in the forest, except for their seeming kindness. So whatever you do, never enter their underground homes. Once inside, they will eat you - slowly ... ripping you apart while you are still alive.'

'That's awful,' Jesse said. She turned on her heel. 'Hurry. Let's get out of this forest.'

'Not so fast,' the wizard said. 'That way leads to the Edge, a fifty thousand feet drop into the gaping jaws of death. Follow me, I know the tricks of this forest well. They've never outwitted me yet.'

'Tis a first time for everything, kind wizard,' Iggywig said. 'Be a-hoping that today is not that day.'

They travelled slowly for almost an hour. The forest watched their every move, waiting for a chance to capitalise on a mistake. When they emerged into the brilliant moonlight of a small clearing, it seemed to Jesse that they had somehow escaped the first part of their journey without any major incidents. But it was a false sense of achievement, for the strangeness of the Skogsra Forest took over.

Round One of *Tracker* was about to begin.

From the stillness of the earth and leaves in the clearing, small shoots pushed out of the soil, green tongues tasting the air. Quickly, they grew into a mass of tangled roots and runners, barbed like wire with teeth and thorns. The speed of their growth surprised Jesse and the others.

The roots and runners slipped like serpents across the earth, entwining themselves around Jesse's ankles. She felt the sharp thorns digging into her flesh, drinking her blood as if vampires.

'It's got me!' she yelled, kicking out.

'Stand still,' Zarlan-Jagr said. 'To struggle will only attract more attention.'

The Dragon Hunter drew his sword and sliced through the roots that were climbing his legs like vines. The roots let out a strange babyish cry, and retracted at lightning speed back into the earth.

'Put your sword away, you fool,' the wizard said. 'Your actions will provoke another attack, even greater than the first.'

He was right. The roots which shot out of the ground now were much thicker and stronger. They arched in the air, wrapping around the Dragon Hunter's arms and legs. He tried to break free, but fell over, hitting the ground hard.

'Tis time to be a-doing something to be a-helping my friends, wizard,' Iggywig said, struggling to fend off a root that was climbing up his leg.

Zarlan-Jagr clapped his hands three times and held out his palms as if surprised or surrendering. Rippling waves of white heat exploded from them like a desert mirage, shimmering and searing. Immediately, the roots screamed, withdrew like withered fingers, turning black and still.

Jesse brushed herself down and helped the Dragon Hunter to his feet. There was a spooky silence around them now.

'Listen carefully,' the Dragon Hunter urged. 'Over there.' He pointed to a small stand of birch-like trees. 'Something moved.'

Round Two: *Tracker.*

'Blast,' the trees yelled. 'You're no fun.'

The stand retreated a few feet, back to their original positions. Jesse blinked in amazement. The trees had unearthed themselves on leg-like roots and shuffled. It was ridiculous, she thought. But this was no laughing matter.

A bush no taller than Jesse suddenly leapt on Iggywig and wrestled him to the ground. 'Come on, you ugly gobrat,' the bush bellowed in a childish voice. 'Give me your best shot. Fight me to the death.'

Iggywig threw the bush off, his face covered in scratches. The mad bush jumped on root-like feet and rammed into Iggywig again, knocking him backwards into the undergrowth. Two ancient gnarled trees whacked out furiously with whipping branches. Iggywig covered his head with his arms and struggled to free himself from the torrent of blows.

Jake hid behind the Dragon Hunter, trembling.

Jesse tried to transform into a raging fire, hoping to burn the attacking trees, but her shape-shifting powers were not working.

'Why can't I shape-shift?' she cried in desperation. She felt the Seeing-Stone in her pocket.

'I don't know,' Zarlan-Jagr said, clapping his hands. He turned the roots and branches, who had pinned Iggywig to the ground, into frozen icicles. 'It doesn't make sense. This is where I learned my natural magical skills. Perhaps you are the victim of a counter-charm to block your shape-shifting.'

'But who would do such a thing?' Jesse asked.

'I can think of many witches and warlocks who would love to counter-charm you, Jesse.'

'Do you think Dendrith and Gwendrith have somehow managed to use their magic from inside the glass egg?' she said.

Zarlan shook his head. 'No. Not possible. But the witch-sisters have many followers and relatives.'

More trees closed in on their position, so that the clearing shrank to half its size. Jesse wasn't sure how the giant trees had moved, because their roots were a blur of whipping and slashing movements.

'Get us out of this forest,' the Dragon Hunter said, raising his sword in a defensive position.

'Before we get out, we have to find Kumo Diaz,' the wizard informed them.

'The tracker who can help us find the New Master of Darkness?' Jesse asked.

'The one and only,' Zarlan-Jagr said with admiration. 'Kumo Diaz is a legend. His knowledge of the inhospitable terrain of the Kingdom of Caldazar is second to none. He's a living legend. Of course, there are some who are dead who know more, but ghosts are notoriously unreliable.'

'Where do we find this Kumo Diaz?' the Dragon Hunter asked.

Zarlan-Jagr shrugged. 'Somewhere in this forest maybe.'

'M-maybe?' Jake said, his eyes darting nervously around him.

The wizard nodded slowly. 'Not only is he the best at finding people, but he's also the best at disappearing in the wilderness.'

'So ... he might not be in the Skogsra Forest?' Jesse said.

'Maybe. Maybe not.'

'So ... what you're really saying is Kumo Diaz could be anywhere in the entire Kingdom of Caldazar - right?'

'Anywhere? Not quite.'

'Meaning?'

'He most certainly will not be in the city of Caldazar. He hates people and crowds of creatures. He prefers his own company. He's a loner - very grouchy and grumpy and hard to get on with.'

'Great,' Jake sighed. 'This is just great. We're looking for a man who d-doesn't want to be found, who hates people, and who is a misery guts into the bargain.'

'Tis an interesting combination this Kumo be a-having,' Iggywig said, nodding. There was laughter in his eyes, even though he kept a straight face.

'What made you think that Kumo Diaz would be here in this vile forest?' the Dragon Hunter wanted to know.

'He likes to play *Tracker* in this place,' the wizard said, motioning at the forest, seeming not to notice that the trees were sneaking in closer and closer.

'He enjoys b-being chased by vicious trees?' Jake asked.

The wizard nodded. 'Kumo Diaz is a fascinating character. And Jake?'

Jake looked expectantly at the wizard. 'Yes?'

'He's not a man.'

'What is he then?' he said hesitantly.

'Kumo Diaz is a ...'

The trees grabbed out, taunting them. They were clearly not giving in.

'Which way now?' the Dragon Hunter asked. 'We need to get out of here.'

'Stay close behind me,' Zarlan-Jagr said.

The wizard wriggled his fingers and began to slice his arm at the roots and lower branches. Like a magic machete he cut a swath through the forest, until ten minutes later they reached another clearing. The pursuing trees seemed reluctant to step into the clearing.

'Wait,' he ordered. 'Let me deal with the

guardian.'

Jesse gazed around, but could see no one.

Zarlan-Jagr stepped into the clearing and opened his arms. 'Mathillath,' he said to silence the trees, animals and wind. 'I have returned, oh Great Spirit, guardian of this sacred forest, will you give me and my friends safe passage to the Caldazar side?'

The rustling trees hushed. No animal made a sound. The wind died. The silence was electrifying.

Then ...

CRACK!

The leaf-littered earth parted just two feet from the wizard, revealing a dark yawning wound. A beam of narrow blue light shot out of the crack, expanding into an ethereal shape. Jesse could make out wide frog eyes, two small nose holes, and an impossibly broad mouth complete with fangs, but the rest of the guardian was too indistinct to see.

'Greetings guardian of this sacred forest,' Zarlan-Jagr said humbly. 'A gift for you.'

The wizard licked his lips once, and a large table appeared before him. On it, a glorious feast - steaming puddings, roast meats, and vegetables.

'Oh, you rascal, Zarlan, you know my weak spot for organic food,' the spirit roared in a voice so deep that Jesse's body shook. It galloped across to the table, and a huge mouth opened and swallowed the lot in one greedy gulp. The spirit of the forest belched loudly and said, 'That was excellent. What other gifts have you?'

'For you, Mpaza, I have treats galore! But tell me: have you knowledge of Kumo Diaz?'

'Mmmm,' the spirit purred. 'Kumo who did you say?'

'Diaz.'

'I'm feeling very hungry, wizard,' Mpaza said, with a greedy glint in his eye. 'A snack may help me remember this Kumbo-Dazzo fellow.'

'Kumo Diaz - the legendary tracker,' the wizard corrected. 'His name is Kumo Diaz.'

'Whatever,' the spirit said. 'Feed me.'

Zarlan-Jagr licked his lips and a giant bowl of slugs and worms appeared. Mpaza chewed on them greedily, slime oozing from the sides of his mouth.

Jake hurried to the edge of the clearing and vomited.

'Ah, my memory is being jogged. I think I remember Kumbo fellow ... yes ... he's a wizard, you say?'

'A tracker, and his name is-'

'More food. I need more food!'

'Yes, of course. Treats galore!'

'Bring them on, Zarlan,' Mpaza said. 'Feed me!'

The wizard conjured instantly a vast selection of perfect fruits and more tender vegetables and meats. They were piled high on the table.

Mpaza shook his head and thick spit rained down on them. 'What is this? A joke? Have you forgotten how I love my third course, wizard?'

'Forgive me,' Zarlan-Jagr said, licking his lips again.

The food rotted and liquefied, as if a thousand

maggots had been let loose on it. The stench forced Jesse to cover her nose and mouth with her hands. It smelled absolutely revolting. The Dragon Hunter didn't seem to notice. Iggywig rushed to the edge of the clearing, joining Jake, and was violently sick.

'Ah,' Mpaza sighed, satisfied. 'Now this is more like it. Delicious!'

He scoffed down the rotten food greedily, wiping the drool from the sides of his mouth with the back of an indistinct hand.

'You and your friends may pass with my blessing,' he said, his belly inflating like an enormous hot air balloon. He sank down, his back against a tree, and closed his eyes. Within seconds, he was asleep, snoring like a pig.

'Wake him,' Jesse ordered the wizard. 'He didn't tell us about Kumo Diaz.'

'Tis unwise to be a-waking a sleeping guardian spirit,' Iggywig said. 'Be no tellings what he might be a-doing. Heads may be a-sliced off, or bones crushed.'

'Iggywig is right,' the wizard agreed. 'Mpaza will be ravenously hungry after sleeping. I do not wish to be on his menu. Do you, Jesse?'

Jake gulped and clasped Jesse's arm.

'But he didn't keep to his side of the bargain,' she said indignantly. 'It's not fair.'

'Just leave it, Jesse,' Jake said.

'Good advice,' the wizard said. 'We have Mpaza's blessing. That will see us through to the Trading Post. Once there, if Kumo Diaz has been here recently, then the traders and trackers and hunters who visit there will know.'

'Hunters?' Jake said, the colour draining from his face. 'I d-don't like the sound of that.'

'What kind of hunters?' Jesse asked.

'The worst kind,' Zarlan-Jagr said. 'The very worst kind.'

Four

# The Labyrinth

They headed north-west, making good time now that they had Mpaza's blessing. Creatures emerged from the dark undergrowth that had been waiting to attack them and came from behind bushes and trees, and gawked. A seven-foot tall standing stoat-like creature known as an aktoka eyed them hungrily, but did nothing to stop them. Three donkey-sized jarmarkins hopped on powerful hind legs in front of them. They exposed vicious rat teeth, twitched their long noses, tasting the air with long forked tongues. One let out a high-pitched squeal, another croaked, while the third simply stared goggle-eyed. They drooled with wild greedy twinkling eyes, but reluctantly let the travellers walk by.

Jesse was mesmerised by the strange variety of creatures that now slinked out of the forest's shadows. She stopped and craned her neck and saw dozens more, some scurrying through the undergrowth, others swinging amongst the treetops. When she turned back to face her companions, she drew in a sharp breath.

They had gone!

Round Three of *Tracker* started.

'Iggywig? Hunter? Where are you?'

A chilled breeze blew up from the undergrowth and clung to Jesse. She shivered, rubbing her arms.

'It's all right,' a soft voice said to her right, and a beautiful creature stepped out from behind a crooked tree. Its eyes were glittering purple light, and its voice sing-songed like a mother's lullaby. Its curvaceous, slender body shimmered beneath the moonlight. 'I saw which way your friends went. Follow me. We can catch them in no time at all.'

Jesse hesitated. Uppermost in her mind was the wizard's warning about the Skogsra and their powers of deception.

'Who are you?' she quizzed.

'A guardian. Come quickly, before your friends get too far away.'

Jesse did not move. Instead, she tried to transform into a dragon, but her shape-shifting magic still wasn't working. Why wouldn't it work? Hadn't the wizard learned his natural magic here in this forest? Perhaps he was right – a counter-charm from one of Dendrith's hags blocked her. She touched the Seeing-Stone in her pocket and felt reassured. Zarlan had claimed that it had powerful magic gifted to him from the Elders of Elriad. Jesse didn't know a thing about the Elders, but they sounded impressive. She was sure that their magic would be impressive, too. *But a word of warning - use the Seeing-Stone wisely and only when no other course of action can be taken.*

Zarlan's words rang in her ears. Did she really need to use the Seeing-Stone?

'Iggywig? Zarlan? Hunter?' she yelled, her voice croaking a little with tension. 'Where are you?'

'They are this way,' the creature said smoothly. As it turned Jesse was shocked by the creature's fox-like tail. 'But quickly. They will soon be out of the forest and you ... well, let's not think about that.'

Jesse felt her heart hammering hard in her chest. What was it Zarlan had said? You're safe as long as you don't enter a Skogsra's burrow? She blotted out the details about flesh eating and shuddered. She felt very cold and alone in the stark moonlight.

She glanced over her shoulder. Behind her there were all kinds of strange creatures and spirits. Could she still count on Mpaza's blessing? They had looked incredibly hungry. And forwards? She did not know. It was a difficult choice. But the longer she dithered, the further away her friends would be.

Her senses tingling with terror, reluctantly she followed the creature deeper into the forest.

*

Jesse ran to keep up with the creature. It seemed to be gliding without any effort, twisting in between gnarled trunks and finger-like roots. Soon the track vanished completely and the trees became more uniform, creating elegant avenues and tunnels.

'Where are you taking me?' Jesse asked.

'There,' said the creature. 'Didn't you see them?'

'No,' Jesse replied flatly.

'They just went round that corner.'

The arched entrance was magnificently carved with gruesome stone gargoyles, snakes and spiders.

Yes, Jesse thought, as they approached the entrance to a labyrinth of stone, I saw them. Her head felt fuzzy, her mind blurred. Or at least she saw a fleeting glimpse of someone rounding the corner ahead. No, it was Iggywig, she was sure.

'Iggywig!' she called, excited at being reunited. She speeded up, almost sprinting now.

The creature vanished around the first corner of the labyrinth. Jesse followed without caution. The passage was empty. Her footfalls echoed loudly on the stone floor.

When she reached the end, she stopped abruptly, and peered around the corner. Complete emptiness again. Grey granite walls and flag stones stared back at her – hard and cold. Row upon row of grotesque stone gargoyle faces peered down at her.

What should I do now? She wondered. Go backward or forward? She was certain she had seen Iggywig, but surely he would have not continued to run? He was her friend. Friends helped one another. And where were the others?

It was an impossible choice.

She considered the Seeing-Stone for a fleeting second. *Remember: the Calm has been restored in many Kingdoms, to use the Seeing-Stone's power needlessly would tip the balance back again to the Darkness.* Instead, she took a Shindish coin from her pocket and tossed it into the air. There were no heads or tails on the coin, so she chose the smooth side. The other side had a strange symbol embossed on it which looked similar to the rune letter *F*. She chose the smooth side. If she won, she'd turn around and head back. The coin tumbled and hit the floor with a hollow jingle. She glanced at it.

She'd lost.

Reluctantly, Jesse trudged further into the maze. At every turn she expected to be confronted by a host of Skogsra, drooling with hunger, or to be dragged screaming into one of their burrows and eaten alive. Yet the deeper she travelled, the safer she felt. Each twist produced nothing but more boring grey flag stones and high imposing walls. She even got used to the stone gargoyles peering down with hard cold eyes. Every time she called out her friends' names, all she got back was an echo of her own voice.

Then without warning, after fifteen minutes, a cold breeze wrapped itself around her legs and crept silently up towards her throat. She stopped, glanced nervously behind her.

No one was there.

Something was dreadfully wrong, though. The

Skogsra had powerful magic. Zarlan-Jagr had said so himself. Her mind was weakening, she knew. Her head pounded, fuzzy and light. The breeze clung tighter to her throat, choking her. It was hard to think clearly. What was it she should do?

She slumped down to her knees. Trap! Yes, it was a trap. Tricked and trapped. Did the maze lead to a Skogsra burrow? Most certainly. So what to do? Backwards or forwards?

The breeze gripped with icy fingers. Jesse tried hard to prise invisible hands from her throat, but there was nothing to grip.

*Theseus would unravel his jumper and use the trail of wool to help him find his way out of the labyrinth.*

Of course he would, she told herself. But this is not a Greek myth, and I am not a warrior.

*No, but you are a remarkable girl with extraordinary powers. Use them.*

I can't, she thought lamely. They don't work in this forest.

*Are you sure?*

Yes.

*But they worked for the wizard.*

Yes. Some sliver of understanding entered her mind. Perhaps she had been glamoured. With all of her energy, Jesse focused on changing into a swift. Something small and useful. She could fly right over the top of the high stone walls. She had to do it! She could hardly breathe. *Remember: the Calm has been restored in many Kingdoms, to use the Seeing-Stone's power needlessly would tip the balance back again to the Darkness.*

I need to use the Seeing-Stone right now, she screamed inside her head. Something is killing me!

She slid her trembling hand into her pocket and grasped the obsidian as hard as she could. *Think your shape ... see your shape ... say your shape ... be your shape.* She saw swirling lights, pumping, pulsing, felt her blood transmuting into her visualised shape. She was changing! Yes, she was changing!

'Stop her!' hissed a female voice.

'I'm trying, but she's broken through. She's dissolving the spell! Her mind is too strong!' the familiar male voice replied desperately.

'Oh, in the name of all that is foul and wicked, use the Blocking-Charm my mother showed you, you dumb warlock!'

Kildrith and Jagdrith! No, it couldn't be, Jesse thought, as she transformed into the tiny bird. She flew to the top of the wall and perched there, surveying the dark forest beyond the maze. Less than a mile to the north she could see the twinkling lights of Caldazar, its twin spires sucking the reflected light from the moons. In between, the densely packed forest was alive with the rustling and rummaging of dark unseen creatures. Below her, the labyrinth of passages zig-zagged towards a yawning dark hole.

'A Skogsra burrow,' she whispered in horror.

'A Skogsra burrow,' Jagdrith echoed sarcastically, and the young witch hovered up from her hiding place in the heart of the maze.

Jesse's mind lurched. 'You!' she said disbelievingly. 'It was you who blocked my magic.'

'Yes, me,' Jagdrith retorted. 'Who did you expect? Your precious Perigold?'

Jagdrith glided across the top of the stones to Jesse and scowled at her. Uncommonly for a witch, she had a pretty face and long blonde hair. However, she had two revolting features: a colossal hairy wart on the end of her chin that looked like a volcano about to erupt with adolescent puss; and eyes that were covered in slimy brown mucus. She was still blinded by Iggywig's charm. Although a sinister crow sat on her shoulder, and by dark unnatural magic the bird was linked to her mind and senses. She saw the world through the bird's eyes.

Jesse felt sick inside at the sight of Jagdrith's shoulder, which was covered in the crow's white slimy droppings.

'So,' Jagdrith said through gritted teeth. 'What have you done with the ghosts of my mother and her sister?'

'I don't know what you're talking about,' Jesse said without thinking.

*Lying is a talent you should work on, Jesse. You never know when you might need it.* The wizard's words reverberated in her head.

'Liar!' Jagdrith spat, and she rolled her eyes madly beneath the mucus. 'You have them imprisoned.'

Jesse ignored her.

'Where are they?'

'How should I know?' Jesse said, shrugging.

'Don't try to play mind games with me, Jesse de Lacjard,' Jagdrith growled. She pushed her face to within six inches of Jesse's tiny bird face. The crow flapped its wings in protest. 'Tell me where they are.'

'My name is Jesse Jameson, and as I've already said, I don't-'

'Liar!'

'Let me kill her,' a thin reed-like voice said softly behind Jesse.

It was Kildrith, hovering with his billowing cloak fanned out around him. The brim of his wide hat was black. It shaded his papery face, but nothing could shade the deep scars embedded in his flesh.

'Not yet,' Jagdrith said.

'Pity,' he said, the tip of his wand beginning to glow with malicious red. 'I love playing killing games. Hide and seek – now that's my favourite, as well you know, young soothsayer. Why don't you run and hide? I'll count to fifty without peeking. One, two, three ...'

'Enough of this,' Jagdrith cut in. 'You can play your sick games later. First, open up her head so that I can see the secrets that she hides in there.'

But my head is a tiny bird's head, Jesse thought, horrified. It's so fragile. It will be crushed. Are they insane?

'A pleasure,' the warlock said, grinning. He touched a few of the scars on his face absently. 'I think it only fair that you should endure a great deal of pain, soothsayer-child. After all, I will only be returning what you gave to me: constant anguish and nightmares.'

He glanced insanely at Jagdrith and they began to chant together a Spell of Malice and Suffering. Over and over they chorused, their voices getting louder and louder.

'*Eye for an eye ... tooth for a tooth ... opened head for a ruined face!*'

Jesse's mind started to spin. She tried to gather her thoughts, but the spell was too powerful, entering the very depths of her mind. She felt numbed and fought with all her might to fix one coherent image in her mind's eye. She had to fly away!

'*Eye for an eye ... tooth for a tooth ... opened head for a ruined face!*'

Kildrith's wand glowed orange, and from it Jesse watched a slow trickle of mist pouring out to form a swirling spiral. It grew and grew, until purple bolts of light flashed and cracked at its core.

'Now!' yelled Jagdrith. 'Open up her head!'

Her crow cawed its approval.

Jesse saw the swirling orange mist whooshing towards her, but she couldn't move an inch, let alone fly. It was all over, she knew. The pain would be unbearable.

'Now!' came an unknown voice.

Jesse felt herself being clasped in warm hands, rising higher and higher into the sky. The higher she was carried, the clearer her mind became. She looked down below, through the curled fingers of her saviour, and saw the two dots that were Jagdrith and Kildrith. She heard their cursing and swearing, and saw angry, blood-red sparks flying from the warlock's wand.

'It isn't over yet, soothsayer!' she heard Kildrith shouting.

'We will have our revenge!' Jagdrith added. Her crow let out a sinister cry. 'Watch your back, Jesse de Lacjard! WATCH YOUR BACK!'

Five

# The Trading Post

The hands were so large that for a moment Jesse thought she must have been dreaming. Jesse transformed back into her fairy self as she was gently put down outside the Trading Post. She drew in a sharp breath. Looking up, she saw the bent figure of a giant, stooping on one knee, his shiny brown eyes blinking almost in slow motion.

'Zarlan sent I to snatch you,' the giant explained in a lilting voice that was as slow as his huge blinking eyes. 'I be doin' as I be told. I do. Not want to be on the sharp end of the wizard's magic, not I. Do not. No.'

Jesse gawked at the giant, her mouth open wide. He was so monumental that his head was higher than the trees in the Skogsra Forest. As he stood up, he left a deep knee print in the ground, and a blizzard of dust rained from his dirty trousers. Jesse coughed and spluttered, shielding her eyes.

'Ooopps!' bellowed the giant. 'I am sorry. I am. I forget how my giantness can cause a rumpus amongst you liddle folks. I do. Yes.'

Still Jesse could not speak. Now that the giant had stood up, she saw the enormity of him. His skin was black and beautiful, his hair a mass of long dreadlocks. And she could now see that the fingers on both hands were each the size of a tall man.

'Thank you ... er ...' she said anxiously. 'Your rescue came at the right time.'

'As I have said, I be doin' as I be told. I do. Yes.'

The giant turned and began to stride away, each step shaking the ground as if an earthquake had ripped it open.

'What is your name?' Jesse called out.

But the giant didn't seem to hear. He strode away purposefully towards Caldazar, and in less than a minute he was miles away, a shadow in the night.

Jesse looked around her. Creatures were emerging from the Trading Post, ranting on about how lucky they had been to survive an encounter with the giant, a monster of Caldazar itself.

'What magic do you possess, fairy child?' one of the traders asked Jesse. 'That was most impressive.'

'Magic?' Jesse said, confused.

'Yeah, did you see the way she put a spell on the brute and sent him away,' said another, and they crowded around her like a press pack out for an exclusive.

'Tell us how to tame a Caldazarian monster.'

Jesse looked at them with an expression of surprise on her face. All of the creatures gathered around her were no taller than three feet. They resembled multi-coloured goblins, for their heads were bald and striped like rainbows. Tiny tufts of green hair sprouted from their ears and noses, and their eyes were yellow, like sparkling amber.

'There must be some kind of mistake,' she said.

'No mistake to defeat a giant. She's holding out.'

'She's a trader, all right.'

'Name your price.'

'How much do you want for your magic, child?'

'I didn't use magic,' Jesse said defensively. 'The giant simply put me down and walked off.'

'She's stalling.'

'A hard bargainer, too. I like that. Her magic must be very powerful.'

'And expensive.'

'I want it,' said a fat little creature with three heads. It was a different species to the rest. It pushed its way to the front, and thrust out scab-ridden hand. 'Decunda Martadahl.'

Jesse stared for a moment at the disgusting outstretched hand. 'I'm sorry, but I have no magic to sell. The giant just walked away of its own free will.'

'Rubbish,' Decunda Martadahl's middle head scoffed. 'You are just playing for higher stakes. Name your price.'

'But I don't have a price.'

'I'll start the bidding,' said another creature. 'Ten thousand Heckles.'

'Fifteen thousand,' Decunda Martadahl's left head offered.

'Sixteen,' said a voice from the back.

'Seventeen,' said another.

'Twenty thousand Heckles,' Decunda Martadahl's right head said.

An excited whisper rippled through the crowd, which had grown to over a hundred strong.

'But I-'

'Twenty-two thousand,' boomed an offer to her left.

'Thirty thousand,' Decunda Martadahl's middle head said.

'You are bidding for no reason!' Jesse shouted. 'Stop this, please!'

'Once the bid has begun, we must have a sale,' Decunda Martadahl's left head said. 'It's the law. Are you refusing to sell?'

'I haven't anything *to* sell.'

'Then the trading continues,' someone said. 'Thirty five thousand Heckles!'

'Forty,' all of Decunda Martadahl's heads offered, looking slightly anxious at the new heights of the bidding. 'And I'll throw in a Palligonian Witch Brewing Kit – fully guaranteed for two hundred years.'

'One hundred thousand,' came a familiar shout from the back of the crowd.

There was a moment of stunned silence, then

Jesse beamed at the sight. The traders parted grudgingly, as Iggywig, Jake, and the Dragon Hunter pushed their way to her. It was Iggywig who had put in the final bid.

The traders muttered uneasily amongst themselves, and as no one could surpass the one hundred thousand bid, they dispersed. They trudged miserably to the bar inside the Trading Post to get drunk.

'You are a very rich and now powerful creature,' Decunda Martadahl's heads said admiringly to Iggywig. He handed the Gobbit a tiny blue stone. 'If you ever need to buy my services then contact me.'

'What services do you offer?' the Dragon Hunter wanted to know.

'Magical ones. I can hire you a Lavatian Wizard Wanger, or maybe you'll need a Perizarvian Potion Maker? Very useful in a crisis. What about a Toad Turning Talisman? Its slow-release properties mean your enemy will hardly be aware of the change. One evening a handsome young creature, the next morning an ugly old toad! Or perhaps an Invisibility Hat from the Horrizulian Regions?'

'Sounds painful,' Jake joked.

No one laughed.

'Tis kind offerings you be a making,' Iggywig said. 'Tis a pleasure a-meeting you. If we be a-needing your services, then we be a-contacting you.'

Decunda Martadahl bowed extravagantly and hobbled away to the Trading Post, vanishing inside.

\*

'What happened to you?' Jake asked at last.

Jesse told them every minute detail. When she had finished, she noticed that Zarlan was missing.

'Where's Zarlan-Jagr?' she quizzed.

'He left a few minutes before you arrived,' the Dragon Hunter said. 'He claimed he was going to track down Kumo Diaz alone.'

'You don't trust him, do you?' Jesse said, detecting sourness in his voice.

The Dragon Hunter shook his head slowly.

'Any reason?'

'Nothing but a bad feeling about him.'

'But that's illogical,' Jake said. 'He has helped us against Dendrith and her sister. He reunited Jesse with Perigold. He-'

'I know what he has done,' the Dragon Hunter cut in. 'On the face of it he seems a loyal and good ally. But there's something about him I don't feel comfortable with.'

'What exactly?' Jesse wanted to know.

The Dragon Hunter shrugged. 'I wish I knew. Then I could kill him for betraying us.'

Jesse looked towards the dark twin spires of Caldazar. 'What do we do next?'

'Wait until the wizard returns?' Jake said.

'Or maybe we should just continue without him,' the Dragon Hunter said.

''Tis an-unwising move,' Iggywig said. 'Zarlan-Jagr be a great wizard. Be a foolish man who be a-turning his back on such helpings.'

'I think you're right,' said Jesse. 'We have no

reason to mistrust him. Besides, just look around. It's very dark. This kingdom is a dangerous and unknown place. We need all the help we can get if we are to find the New Master of Darkness.'

'So where do we wait?' Jake asked. 'In the Trading Post, or out here in the wilderness?'

*

The Trading Post was crowded. Jesse and Jake had to squeeze between a whole host of remarkable creatures to find the only empty table. While Iggywig and the Dragon Hunter went to the bar to get food and drinks, Jesse sat down heavily on a rickety stool and gazed around.

Blurred within the blue haze of cigarette smoke and wall-mounted oil lamps, Jesse could see strange creatures with necks as long as giraffe's necks, and heads so fat and bulbous that they looked as if they would pop at any moment. There were plump, walrus-type creatures, sitting drunkenly at the bar, laughing loudly and patting each other on ridged backs. She could just make out Iggywig, edging cautiously around a group of creatures who had wide eagle eyes, and arms and legs covered in fish scales. A beautiful, two-nosed creature sat in the corner, playing an instrument that resembled a twisted golden harp. Her voice sounded more like a baby screaming than singing, but the traders applauded and cheered for more every time she finished a song. Everywhere, currency and goods exchanged hands; the rowdiness of bartering grew and subsided, rose and fell.

Jake sat down next to her, looking pale and exhausted.

'Are you all right?' Jesse asked.

'I'm fine,' Jake said. 'Well – kind of.'

'What do you mean?'

'It's ever since the Bogie Beast possessed me – I feel kind of weird inside. It's like I'm dreaming all of this.'

'You don't think some of his black goo is still roaming around inside your body, do you?' Jesse said, trying to sound conversational, but sounding slightly alarmed.

'No!' Jake said defensively. 'I mean, I hope not. That's an awful thought, Jesse.'

'Yes, it is. I'm sorry. But there have been so many strange things happening since I entered the Fairy Kingdoms that – well, it seems anything is possible.'

'Yeah, I know exactly what you mean. Even as we speak, the New Master of Darkness could be in here somewhere, and we wouldn't even know it.'

Jesse shuddered. 'Cut it out, Jake. What would he be doing in here?'

'Watching us, maybe. Waiting for the right moment to strike.'

'Very funny.'

'You said yourself that anything was possible in the Fairy Kingdoms.'

'Yes, I did, it's as if our worst nightmares keep manifesting.'

'Yeah, this is a mad place all right.'

There was a moment of silence between them.

A glass smashed somewhere out of sight. The traders cheered.

'You could have gone home, you know,' Jesse said at last. 'I would have taken you back to the human world.'

Jake reached out slowly and touched Jesse's hand across the table. 'I wanted to be with you.'

Jesse blushed and withdrew her hand.

'You once said I was mad, Jake Briggs. But I think you're the mad one.'

'Why is that?'

'You must miss your mum and dad, school, and-'

'Of course I do, but if I go back I'll ...'

He stared starry-eyed at her.

'You'll what?'

'Oh, it doesn't matter,' Jake said dismissively. 'Look, here come the others with food and drink. It looks good. I'm starving.'

'You'll what?' Jesse persisted.

'Oh – nothing. It doesn't matter. Another time, Jesse,' Jake said tersely, and he got up and helped Iggywig and the Dragon Hunter.

Six

# Kumo Diaz

As the skies outside darkened further still, the Trading Post door crashed open. The blue-white flash of Caldazarian weapon fire momentarily lit up behind two silhouetted figures. The door slammed shut. Zarlan-Jagr and his companion stood there, wide-eyed and shaking. They scanned the room.

Jesse was already on her feet, rising to greet them.

'Stay down!' Zarlan-Jagr commanded. He leapt to pull Jesse to the ground as the windows exploded.

Jake, Iggywig, and the Dragon Hunter dived under a table, glass and brick rubble showering them. Some traders mirrored them, but not all. A handful wrenched open the door, managed to slam it shut and ran straight into the lethal, silent weapon fire of the Caldazarian soldiers.

Jesse covered her ears, trying to block out their

screams.

Silence. Flashes of blue-white weapon fire illuminated the room, but no sound. It was like being part of a bizarre silent movie, Jesse thought.

Another window exploded. She covered her head with an arm, shaken from her shock. Glass showered her. She shook it off as best she could.

'Are you Kumo Diaz?' Jesse said, studying the strange small tracker.

The thin, black-faced creature blinked slowly. He had one, huge fly-eye in the middle of his wide forehead. He sniffed and snuffled the air with a long, pointed mole-like snout.

'Like a butterfly, we are caught in a net, surrounded on all sides. The Caldazarian soldiers will soon break down the door to this pathetic hovel. We must hurry. This way,' he said, as if he had been awoken from a deep hibernation and begrudged the intrusion.

Motioning for Jesse and her friends to follow him, Kumo Diaz led the way behind the Trading Post's bar. On hands and knees, they crawled rapidly across the filthy floor. They ducked behind the bar as more windows exploded. Within moments, the cellar door had been opened and closed, with all of them safely inside. They descended the stairs rapidly.

The cellar was dark and smelled damp and mouldy. Muffled cries and more exploding windows could be heard above them. They found a tiny entrance in the far wall, behind a stack of barrels. They squeezed through and crawled along a series of narrow tunnels. Jesse tried to ignore the cobwebs clinging to her hair and face.

'Clathdor!' Zarlan-Jagr said, and a secret entrance opened ahead of them. The tip of the wizard's staff glowed a soft orange light, casting spooky shadows on the rough earth walls. A thin wafer of purple smoke rose from the tip.

At least now they could stand. They journeyed without talking, puffing and panting for breath in the half-lit stifling air.

After five minutes, they were deep into the maze of passages. It was then that Jesse stumbled, staggered, and fell awkwardly to the cobbled floor.

'What's wrong?' the Dragon Hunter cried in alarm.

Zarlan-Jagr pushed his way to Jesse's side. As the wizard held his glowing staff closer to her body, the companions gasped in horror: Jesse had been shot – badly.

*

As soon as Jesse hit the floor darkness crept over her. She was falling into a never-ending well of black. Awash with pain her world faded in and out of view. It was so intense that she blanked out. Visions came - moonbeams slicing between strange falling planets. She was a star, a cat and a mouse, an exploding super nova, a galaxy imploding into a black hole, transforming into a hideous monster, dragons of red, blue, green and white, a giant whale, a yellow balloon, a wooden peg, a turtle.

'I have ridden shooting stars and I will show you how,' she heard herself say.

Surge upon surge of unbearable pain ripped at her insides. Her mother's face came and went – and so too did the nightmare of the Bogie Beast.

Then, stillness. Time stopped. The dark space was vast and empty of everything.

Suddenly there came the terrifying vision of a witch stuck in ice, screaming and wailing revenge.

Jesse tried to turn her head away from the horror, but it was no use. The witch's will forced her to watch as each splash of freezing water fell, instantly turning into another serrated tooth of ice. The riverbed was a vast mass of gleaming teeth that extended high into the clouds, trapping the witch.

Like a camera lens zooming-in at speed, the High Witch, Zundrith, came sharply into view.

'Am I dead?' Jesse said, already sure of the answer.

Zundrith the High Witch stared without expression into Jesse's eyes, drinking her in.

'Very soon,' she thought she heard the witch hiss, but something else grabbed her attention. A cold ripple of horror scraped down her spine. There was some-one tapping on her shoulder. She blinked and saw Iggywig and Jake. But it was hopeless. She was dragged back into Zundrith's aura with a force like a magnet ripping up iron-filings.

'So glad you could return, you pathetic brat. Now let go of that golden glow so that I may bottle it the same way you bottled my Sisters in Suffering. Let go - now!'

The power of what came next smashed Jesse in

her stomach. She doubled over in pain. She tried to scream but no sound came out. She staggered backwards … one … two … three short steps. It felt as if something precious had been wrenched from her. She knew she had lost her golden glow.

*

Jesse couldn't open her eyes, but she heard the bizarre conversation.

'Are they sealed?' Zarlan-Jagr said.

'Yes,' confirmed Kumo Diaz.

'Check, please. She mustn't see a thing. The magic is far too powerful. One glimpse, no matter how small, would blind her.'

'Be a very awesome magic you be a-making, kind wizard.'

'Stand back, please,' Zarlan said.

Jesse felt cold sticky fingertips on her eyelids.

'Yes, they're sealed,' said Kumo Diaz.

'Look away everyone,' Zarlan ordered.

'Be a-good advising.'

Jesse heard Jake and the Dragon Hunter muttering and there was a scuffling of boots and shoes on dirt. She could smell the earthiness of the tunnel, and guessed they hadn't moved her. The pain of her wound raged now like a firestorm. She opened her mouth to scream. A warm, soft hand clamped over it. The scream was muffled.

'Now!'

Even with her eyes sealed like tombstones Jesse saw the flash of bright golden light. The sound of sizzling and the pungent aroma of burning flesh came briefly, then …

Even though she knew it was her flesh being healed from the inside out, she found herself floating above her body.

She looked down at the scene below. All of her companions were turned with their backs to her. Iggywig was holding Jake's hand. Jake was sniffling, shaking his head. Fear was etched on his face like a linocut.

Jesse floated down and spoke to Jake, but he couldn't hear her. She reached out to comfort him, but her hand passed through his face.

'Oh, no!' she yelled. 'Oh, please, God. No!'

But she knew with a growing alarm and horrifying certainty that she was dead!

Beyond the scene, Zundrith appeared. She was smiling, although her twisted smile looked like a scowl of pain.

'No,' Jesse said limply. She shook her head and swallowed hard. 'My glow. Give it back!'

Zundrith clutched the bottle containing Jesse Jameson's golden glow. She raised it like a trophy above her head and shook it.

'Mine!' she roared. 'Mine!'

'Give it back!'

'Goodbye, you little brat,' the witch said, and she folded inside herself and started to disappear. 'Thank you.' She paused and flashed her cold eyes dramatically. 'Thank you ... so much.'

\*

The Dragon Hunter span round quickly. He dropped to his knees and cradled Jesse's limp head in his strong hands.

'No!' he roared. 'Jesse!'

Jake couldn't bear to look. He slumped forward against the wall and buried his sobbing face in his arms.

Iggywig seemed incredibly confused. His belief in magic was so immense that to witness its failure was impossible to understand. He was shocked, unable to move.

'You said it would work, wizard,' Kumo Diaz said. 'But she is dead. Your magic is a fool's magic. You are a phoney.'

'Please, my friends, let's not be hasty,' Zarlan-Jagr said calmly. 'Let the magic take its course. Like lightning it must travel its route, and find an earth. Once it has found the source of the wound it *will* work.'

'Iggywig be a-praying to the good Lord Boeron.' The gobitt dropped to his knees, closed his eyes, and began to pray.

A golden tear dropped from the Dragon Hunter's eye and landed on Jesse's cheek. The tear rolled slowly like molten lava down her face.

'Bring her back, wizard,' the Dragon Hunter yelled, twisting up to glare at Zarlan-Jagr. 'Otherwise you will swiftly follow her to the afterlife.'

'My friends – please keep your faith.'

Kumo Diaz put the back of his hand close to Jesse's lips. 'She has no breath. She is dead.'

'I'm not dead,' Jesse said. 'Do you hear me? I'm alive. I'm here. Look!'

She waved her arms in front of Kumo Diaz's

face, but he was unaware of her.

'Iggywig. Jake. Dragon Hunter!'

She waved at them frantically.

No response.

Jesse glanced down at herself, lying motionless and grey on the hard stony earth.

'It doesn't look like me,' she said. She thought about a school visit she had gone on. Madame Tussaud's in London had waxwork models of famous people. 'I look like a wax doll.'

Without warning, she felt a tug on her hand. She looked down and saw a small ghostly quargkin.

'Pleased to meet you, Jesse Jameson,' the quargkin said. 'My name is ...'

'Bantrash!'

'Yes – how did you know that?'

'I was there at Alisbad City when you were ... how should I put it?'

'Killed and eaten by a dopey fat troll.'

Jesse laughed. 'Yes. It was horrible.'

'Yes – it was. Being munched by that monster was no picnic, I can tell you.'

'You must have suffered terrible pain.'

'Not really. Just like you – I found myself out of my body in no time at all.'

'So I *am* dead then?'

'Fraid so, Jesse. But not for long.'

Jesse looked puzzled. 'What do you mean?'

'You'll see. And I'll see you later – maybe.'

'And maybe not,' Zundrith hissed, reappearing again in a cloud of white snow.

\*

It happened all at once, a kind of pulling sensation in the pit of Jesse's stomach. At the same time, Zundrith screamed as the bottle containing the golden glow melted in her scrawny hand.

'No!' the High Witch yelled. 'I need that! Give it back to me now!'

Jesse watched as Zarlan-Jagr wriggled his fingers. He pointed at the witch and with a flick of his wrist unleashed an unseen force that hit her like a wave. She shot backwards into a void that opened behind her. For a brief second Jesse saw jagged ice teeth and frozen barren wastelands, a solid twisted river, and ... the witch travelling backwards, her arms and legs and hair thrashing wildly to that terrible place. The void closed with a crack.

She was gone.

It was then that Jesse felt herself lurching forward, tumbling toward her body. It was like being sucked down a funnel. A second later she was thumped in the stomach. Her golden glow returned with great force.

Bang!

A shaft of zigzagging light bounced off the walls and then there came an awful darkness. Jake, Iggywig and the rest vanished from her ghostly sight. Darkness.

'Wake her,' Kumo Diaz said.

'Let her rest,' Zarlan-Jagr whispered. 'Leave her eyes sealed until she is ready to accept the prospect of her new self.'

Jesse felt very scared by what she heard. What

did the wizard mean by 'accept the prospect of her new self?' What in Boeron's name had they done?

\*

When Jesse woke and opened her eyes, the first thing she saw was Iggywig. His broad cheeky grin greeted her. Jake stood against the dimly lit wall of the tunnel, smiling like the Dragon Hunter.

'What's wrong?' Jesse said. 'What's happened to me?'

Zarlan and Kumo Diaz stepped into her view.

'There is no easy way to say this, Jesse,' Zarlan-Jagr admitted. 'So ... brace yourself for a shock.'

Zarlan wriggled the fingers of his left hand and from nowhere appeared a small mirror. He offered it to Jesse.

She hesitated for a moment.

'Be a-wonder to behold, Jesse Jameson,' Iggywig said softly. 'Tis a blessing that we both be changed.'

'Is it bad?' Jesse said, her voice cracking. 'You can tell me. The truth.'

'Tis as it be – neither good nor bad, or perhaps both. Tis Jesse who must be a-deciding.'

'Please don't talk in riddles.'

'Tis true – look.'

Iggywig took the mirror from Zarlan and held it up so that Jesse could see. She laughed out loud – a hollow belly laugh that echoed along the dark tunnels.

'I look the same,' she said. 'What's the problem?'

'That's the good,' Jake said. He walked over to Jesse and stood beside her. 'But there's something else.'

'What?' she said, narrowing her eyes. She'd seen that 'Jake face' hundreds of times in class. It was hard to describe, a kind of playful knowing - all in one fleeting expression.

'Feel anything different yet?' he said, holding her upper arm as way of support.

'No. Why? Should I?'

Jake nodded.

'Tis a-coming like a rockulator,' Iggywig said, holding Jesse's other arm.

'Let go. What are you two doing?'

Jesse firmly removed Jake's grip from clenching the flesh of her arm. Then something odd happened. She felt a wave of heat travel from her feet to her stomach. A freezing sensation swiftly followed from her head to her neck. She shuddered, coughed involuntarily, and began to shake like a rickety building in an earthquake. Golden lights revolved before her eyes. Her friends came and went out of her vision. She toppled. She made a grab, but Jake and Iggywig steadied her.

'What's happening?' she hollered, panicked.

'You are changing,' Zarlan said. 'Let your new powers through. Don't fight them. The Seeing-Stone will guide and protect you.'

'Shape-shifting, you mean?'

'No – you're in the middle of a magical transformation.'

'Magical?'

'Yes. You now have what we call a Magiceye.'

'Like a light meter, you mean?'

'A what?'

'Oh, never mind. I think I understand.' But she didn't really. Inside she was terribly afraid. Magiceye? What had happened to her?

'Look. She's transforming,' Kumo Diaz said.

'Into what?' Jesse said, doubling with a bolt of pain that hit her from nowhere in her solar plexus.

'A fairy child with new magic in her eyes,' Kumo Diaz said.

She groaned, a vast surge of heat and cold hitting her forehead. Her legs buckled, she writhed in pain, clutching her pounding head. She sank to her knees. But then, as quickly as it came it was gone – all painful sensations faded.

Calm.

Iggywig gave her the mirror. What she saw bemused her. Her eyes were kaleidoscopes of colour, but more than this she could see bright fizzing colours around her friends.

'Remarkable, isn't it?' Zarlan said.

'What are the bands of colour I see around everyone?'

'Cocoons of light. You see the eternal life-force in which a person is immersed.'

'Your words sound like a foreign language to me.'

'With this new gift of auric sight, you will be able to know many things.'

'Like what exactly?'

'The colours of light around living things show

you their health, their thoughts, their desires. Once you learn to understand what each colour means then you will know a great deal about the person. For instance, you will able to tell whether or not someone is lying to you.'

'Cool,' said Jake.

'Is it really cool?' Jesse looked at Jake's aura, streaked around his head with hints of green. Something inside her said that he was jealous of her new powers.

'Sure it's cool,' Jake said. 'It would be great to know stuff about someone without them knowing.'

Jesse resisted the urge to say that she knew how Jake really felt about her new gift.

'Fine,' she said. 'You be me. Let's swap.'

'I wish I could,' Jake said.

'No you don't. You have no idea how horrible this is.' And she thought: I know how you feel about my new gift, Jake. You are so jealous, but I can't tell you because you'll be upset that I know what you think.

'You are growing magically,' Zarlan said. 'It is a difficult time. But remember the Seeing-Stone. It can give you understanding and guidance.'

Jesse buried her head in her hands. 'I just want to be the way I was before. Doesn't anyone see that?'

'But it's not that much different,' Jake said. 'I think it's a lot like knowing for certain about your hunches and intuitions, isn't it Zarlan?'

'Well put, Jake.' The wizard smiled kindly.

Jesse shielded her eyes from the wizard's

blinding white aura. 'Too much power, too much magic.'

'I will teach you how to tune-out people's auras, Jesse,' the wizard said. He came to her and cupped his soft hands to her ear. He whispered one single magical word to turn off the gift: 'Brathllall.' And then another word was whispered to turn the Magiceye on again: 'Tuyanahey.'

'In my mind or out loud?' she said.

'Never out loud. It is for your ears only. Try it.'

In her mind she spoke the ancient word *brathllall* and her eyes turned blue once more and the auras faded. It was such a relief. But she still felt odd.

'I'm a freak,' she said at last.

'You're not a freak,' Zarlan said. 'You're just different. The trick of magic is learning when and how to use it to serve your needs, or the needs of others. Don't be so hard on yourself. The Seeing-Stone will guide you. Remember: you are just different.'

'I know,' she said. 'That's what I keep finding out. First a fairy swapped at birth with a human child, then a soothsayer and a shape-shifter, and now this – a Magiceye who can see other people's aura, know things about their health, thoughts, and desires before they do.'

'Cool,' Jake said.

'Grow up, Jake,' Jesse scolded. 'You have no idea how much responsibility this new gift brings with it.'

'No,' Jake said. 'I don't know. I'm sorry.'

'I don't want your pity. I just want to be the old me – just plain Jesse Jameson.'

They travelled in silence through the tunnels. There was nothing anyone could say.

Seven

# Shadow Eaters

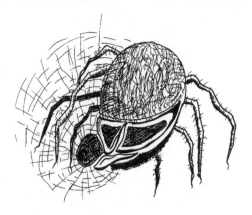

When they emerged from the earth, Jesse and her companions fell silent. Before them rose Caldazar - a vast, expanding mass of dark granite mountain, sharp needles of rock, jagged plateaus, spikes of smooth, hard stone. Miles of fortification stood between them and the inner city. There was no way through.

'This is where it ends,' the Dragon Hunter said, turning to head back into the tunnel.

Zarlan-Jagr clasped the Hunter's arm. 'Wait,' he said firmly. 'There is a way.'

'Be not a-wising to fly,' Iggywig said. He motioned above the defences to the east. The sky was crammed with giant winged beasts.

'Like a swarm of locusts they patrol the skies above Caldazar,' Kumo Diaz explained.

'What are they?' Jake asked timidly. He gulped at the sight, which he was certain was heading in their direction.

'Baalvosh,' Zarlan hissed. 'Quickly, let's hide.'

'Hide?' The Dragon Hunter's sword of light swished from its scabbard and hummed a deep resonant note. 'I will die fighting.'

'Yes,' said Kumo Diaz. 'You will.'

'Goodbye.' Zarlan-Jagr said, patting the Hunter on his back, and he led them away towards the River Stark.

'Wait for me,' Jake said, hurrying to join the wizard and the tracker.

'Cowards,' the Hunter spat. 'See how your friends desert you?'

Jesse smiled and shook her head.

'They are not cowards,' she defended. 'They can see, as I can, that we are out-numbered ten thousand to one.'

'Be a no timing for a-chitter chattering,' Iggywig reminded them. 'Hurry.'

'I am tired of running away,' the Dragon Hunter said. 'It goes against all I believe.'

'I know,' Jesse agreed. It was an old song the Dragon Hunter sang, and Jesse was getting tired of it. 'But even you must see that this is not the time to stand and fight.'

The Dragon Hunter glanced up at the dark clouds of Baalvosh, then back to Jesse.

'For you, and no one else, I will hide, Jesse Jameson.'

'We are not hiding,' she said, following the others - Iggywig and the Hunter in tow. 'It only seems that way.'

The Dragon Hunter grunted something offensive. Iggywig laughed.

'It's a long time since Iggywig be a-hearing that swear word.'

'Karghoffmuck,' the Dragon Hunter growled again.

'What does it mean?' Jesse said.

'Best not be a-knowing, young Jesse. For your ears it be not allowing.'

Shame, thought Jesse, and she quickened her pace to join the others.

The Baalvosh swarmed closer.

\*

A few minutes later a young blonde witch with a crow on her foul shoulder and an ape-like warlock appeared from the tunnel and glanced up at the sky.

'Which way?' Jagdrith said, licking her lush lips hungrily.

Kildrith tipped back the brim of his storm-coloured hat with a bony malformed finger. He studied the mass of towering rock, the approaching Baalvosh, and then scanned the narrow pathway to his left. He sniffed the rancid air, which smelled of burning metal.

'She is close, the soothsaying scum.'

'So? Which way?' Jagdrith said, clenching her fist. The crow scanned the landscape nervously.

'Don't rush me, witch child,' Kildrith snapped. 'My nose is not as it used to be since Jameson set her magic upon me. Just look at my ruined face.'

He turned so that silver moonlight lit up the

full horror of his wounds.

'Save the sob story for the Warlocks' Reunion, Kildrith. Get over it. You were no beauty before the damage. Now, which way?'

'Witches,' Kildrith cursed. 'All heart and no golden glow.'

'Shut up and find the soothsayer.'

Kildrith's broken mouth attempted a grin. He knew the golden glow episode hurt.

'So?'

'This way, witch child,' he groaned. He pointed to the pathway where Jesse and her companions had hurried. 'They went down there less than five minutes ago.'

A few wasps spewed from Jagdrith's mouth, flew around her tall black hat. Sensing the danger above, they slipped back inside their mistress' mouth. The crow flapped its shiny wings fretfully.

'Don't worry, my little pretties,' she reassured them. 'The Baalvosh will not worry us. We are too dark for their weak eyes. They seek the light of our enemies. Their golden glows grow stronger every day. How boring to be so pure and good and sanctimonious.'

Jagdrith spat disdainfully.

'Are you ready, witch child? Or would you like more time to baby-talk your damned wasps?'

'Shut it,' Jagdrith said. 'When I want your opinion, I'll ask for it.'

Kildrith laughed. 'So much like your mother and aunt,' he said sarcastically.

'Don't forget it, warlock.' She narrowed her

pretty mucus eyes to menacing slits. Instantly they changed colour: blood red.

'How can I? All you talk about is your precious Dendrith's revenge and getting that damned glass egg!'

*

As the High Witch, Zundrith, hugged to the shadows, she muttered incantations and curses into the perpetual waterfall. Every splash of freezing water tumbled and turned into another icy fang. The riverbed was a mass of glimmering teeth which reached into the clouds. It always grew and never melted. Though she desired more than life itself to move – just a single step – she was rooted to the river bank like an ancient tree. Yet, she knew who had tricked her, cursed her, charmed her; who had enslaved her for almost a thousand years. Not long now, she told herself for the countless time, it would not be long before she would be free. Soon, yes soon, there would be chaos, butchery and every sea and river would run with blood.

'One day soon, my pathetic little retinue,' Zundrith hissed. 'I shall climb this mountain of ice and teeth and blood and bones. I shall conquer this blasted summit, and free you all. Yes! We will crush our enemies and all who stand in our way. But ... not before I have my revenge for the sisters held in that damn glass egg!'

It was an old speech, but she knew it well. It comforted her like a heartbeat comforted a baby.

In the palm of her open hand, a tiny red creature came to life. She whispered to the creature harshly, a language unkind and stinging. She licked her upper lip and grimaced with sick pleasure. She spat on the creature. She studied it through squinting black eyes as the tiny grotesque thing morphed into a replica of herself. She hissed and it sprouted wings and a corkscrew of rhino horn in the middle of its forehead.

'Fly, my little demon. Do my bidding. Find them. Crush them. Suck the lifeblood from their veins,' she ordered. 'Now!'

Her body juddered and she bayed woefully, urging others from the icy wastelands of the Monstrous Mountains. Tens of thousands flew rapidly. Dark shapes glided in and out of view. They were knotted around the folds of her cloak, lazed around in the unnatural nightfall that surrounded her. They gathered up the winged demon and helped it on its way – screaming.

'Go, my pretties,' Zundrith cackled. 'Go now and destroy them, but bring the fairy child, Jesse Jameson, to me.'

As the hoardes of eddying demons did her bidding, her brother, Dumdrith, appeared from the shadows beside her. He was wet and dripping purple goo as usual.

With frightening speed he flicked his neck. Cracking bone and sinew at the base of his skull a mouth, with rotten gnashing incisors, opened between tangled red hair. A black tongue slithered out, and a newly-born bat appeared. It slipped into his hand like thick custard from a bowl.

'For me, dear brother?'

Dumdrith nodded stupidly. He presented the bat to her, afraid to look anywhere but her webbed feet.

Zundrith cackled as she pressed the bat in her fingers. She unhinged her jaws and flashed row upon row of razor teeth.

'I'm starving! Give me more of what you have stored in your head, brother! Feed me now!'

*

Jesse hurried behind Zarlan-Jagr, keeping as close as possible. They travelled a few hundred yards up a narrow, sloping path. The rocks beneath their feet hampered progress. They slipped and slid, fell, got up again, at last they climbed to the ridge. Below them they could see the vast River Stark, black and steaming. It meandered like a great lightless snake. Caldazar stood high above – bleak, ruthless, and dark.

'Now what?' Jesse said.

'There's no way over it,' Kumo Diaz said. 'Not even by boat. If we had one – which we do not.'

'Do we fly?' Jake asked.

Zarlan motioned to the approaching cloud of Baalvosh. 'Only a fool would fly.'

Jesse shuddered. The dark cloud reminded her of the clouds of flying monkeys in the *Wizard of Oz*. Only this cloud of creatures were ten times larger.

'We go underground,' Kumo Diaz said, leading them down a winding track, towards the River.

'Not again.' Jake groaned. 'I hate the dark.'

'Tis a bad omen Iggywig be a-seeing,' the gobbit piped up. 'Look.'

They gawked at the wet, red scrap of cloth Iggywig dangled in his hand. 'Be fresh.'

'Fresh what?' Jesse asked.

'Blood,' the Dragon Hunter said, taking the cloth and offering it to Jesse.

She shook her head and backed away. 'No thanks,' she said. 'I believe you. Whose blood?'

'Probably the most recent travellers who tried to gain access to Caldazar through the catacombs.'

'What are the catacombs?'

'A maze of tunnels, where many dead are stored,' Zarlan said. They halted as they reached the dark entrance. 'These catacombs are populated by the living also - shadow creatures. Blood suckers. Flesh eaters.'

'Hold on a minute,' Jesse said, grabbing Zarlan's arm. 'Blood sucking Shadow Eaters?'

The wizard nodded, then smiled. 'Not scared are you?'

'Of course I'm scared.'

'Good,' he said. 'You should be. The Shadow Eaters are awesome hunters. They can sniff a shadow a mile away.'

'But blood? That sounds absurd. There isn't blood in a shadow, is there?'

Zarlan nodded. 'Enough to feed the Shadow Eaters.'

'But that doesn't sound so bad,' Jesse said, considering the idea. 'What pain is there in losing your shadow?'

'For humans, none whatsoever. Their shadows are bloodless.'

He glanced at Jake and smiled.

'Why don't I feel pain if I lose my shadow?' Jake asked them, sounding wounded.

'It's a long story,' Zarlan said. 'Maybe another time I'll tell you about the Far-Seeing Shadow Legend.'

'Tis a tale to be a-telling,' Iggywig said. 'But Zarlan be a-righting. No time.'

'And fairy people?' Jesse butted in. Her voice was tinged with anxiety. 'What kind of pain?'

'The worst kind of pain imaginable, Jesse,' Kumo Diaz added.

'Look out!' the Dragon Hunter yelled.

A dozen or so Baalvosh swooped down and clawed at the group. The Dragon Hunter released his sword of light, swinging left and right. But the Baalvosh were masters of the air. They swooped and dived, squealing as though a life time of death and despair had been imprisoned inside them and had just been released.

Jesse covered her ears, but the death wail entered her mind, ran like quick-silver down her spine, and filled her bones, blood and skin.

'Hurry!' Someone amongst them yelled. 'This way!'

Jesse was jostled into the depths of the catacombs, hands still locked like wheel clamps to her ears. She screamed. Iggywig screamed. She saw Jake fall to his knees, bury his head in his hands, screaming into the dust.

An explosion of pink-blue light. It invaded the dark, lit up the catacombs for a split second. With the new darkness came silence.

Jesse heard Jake sobbing, but that was all. No, not all. There was a drip, drip, drip of water somewhere ahead in the dark. She glanced up to see the vestiges of Zarlan's magic returning into his fingertips. Pink-blue light rippled like water breaking onto the shore of a lake. It reminded her of a family holiday she'd had up at the Lake District: happy, secure, warm. Her brief memory of her mum and dad came and went in a flash. She longed to be with them again. But her stark reality swam into view.

The drip, drip, drip continued in the gloom ahead of them.

'No time to waste,' Zarlan said. 'We will split up to double our chances of reaching Caldazar.'

'Is that wise?' the Dragon Hunter said.

'Yes,' said Kumo Diaz. 'I'll lead you and Jake via the Smourleaf Path. I know it well. It's not an easy journey. It's long but with luck we can be inside Caldazar before breakfast.'

'I'll take Jesse and Iggywig,' Zarlan added, pointing. From his finger, a ray of light shot out like a torch beam and illuminated a ridge above them. 'We'll take the Dmourlagen Path. It's narrow and hard to climb, but it's quicker.'

'Let's go. Good luck,' Kumo Diaz said.

And before anyone had time to think about protesting, Kumo and Zarlan hurried along each separate path, leading the way into the depths of darkness.

'See you in Caldazar,' Jake shouted. 'Bet we

can get there first.'

'I bet you can, Jake,' Jesse said. 'See you there.' She just didn't feel good about them splitting up, but she was too tired to protest. She would just have to trust Zarlan and Kumo to lead them safely into the teeming city of monsters.

Their own shadows leapt and lurked up the curved cave walls. Zarlan's lighted finger shone like a bright torch. They struggled higher and higher up the slippery rocky path for hours. The air was icy cold now, and it smelled stale and old. It was no easy climb, but they plodded on.

'This is madness,' Jesse muttered. She tried not to look into the catacomb chambers, each with their wrapped and mummified dead. 'Complete madness.'

'Tis best not to be a-thinking far ahead, kind Jesse,' Iggywig said. 'Too much a-brooding on the what ifs be a-bad for the brain.'

Iggywig was right, of course, Jesse thought, keeping close to him. But no matter how hard she tried, she couldn't block the monsters of Caldazar from her mind.

Somewhere in the bowels of the catacombs, the flesh eating shadow creatures prowled. Waiting. Watching. Whispering. High above the catacombs, the Baalvosh flew, tracking them with magical means only they understood.

As she climbed higher into the vast tunnels and along narrow, twisting pathways, Jesse considered the events since arriving in the Unknown Kingdoms. The Rumble had made clean all of Troth and Finnigull, but its force had not touched this land, had it? She wondered why. Her mind remained a blank. And what of the Union of Thirteen? The thought of Perigold as some kind of secret wizard pledged to fight evil really was incredible. She was still dumbfounded by the revelation, but was more concerned about finding a cure for her grandfather. She shook her head. She found the idea of Perigold as her real grandfather astonishing. But she felt warmed by it. She loved him. And what of Zarlan-Jagr and his gifts from the Elders of Elriad – the Seeing-Stone and the Magiceye? Her magical powers were growing quickly and the thought of them and the great responsibility which came with them scared her.

Eventually the catacombs opened up into a large cavern. A small pool of water, the size of a manhole cover, radiated a golden light from its edges.

Fascinated, Jesse hurried over to the pool. It was still and reflected the roof some fifty feet above. The walls and the roof reminded Jesse of black shiny coal.

'Don't touch it or look into it, whatever you do,' Zarlan-Jagr said, placing his hand on her shoulder.

'I wasn't going to,' Jesse said, feeling annoyed that the wizard thought that she could be so thoughtless.

'Then why run so quickly to see it?'

'I don't know,' she admitted, not taking her eyes from the pool's gleam.

'You feel a strong attraction to it, don't you?'

'Yes.' She shrugged away his hand. 'Now leave me alone.'

'As you wish,' Zarlan-Jagr said. 'But don't you want to know what lurks beneath the water?'

Jesse couldn't drag her eyes away.

'Not really,' she said. 'I feel safe here.'

'Tis a powerful glamour Jesse be a-feeling,' Iggywig said. He went to her and gripped her upper arm. 'Be best if we be a-continuing on our journeyings.'

Jesse shrugged off Iggywig's hand. 'You go ahead. I'll catch you up.'

'No, Jesse,' Zarlan said firmly. 'Come with me now before the Drakmire enters your mind more deeply. It has already taken hold. Remember the Skogsra Forest? Well, the Drakmire work for the Shadow Eaters. They are trying to control your mind, to slow us all down, so that the Shadow Eaters can catch us and have their fill.'

'But it's so beautiful,' Jesse said, instantly forgetting the wizard's words. 'So still and peaceful.'

She sighed.

'No, Jesse. Tis an illusioning. Please be on our way.'

'Yes,' Zarlan said. 'Iggywig is right. And we are not far from the exit which leads to Caldazar.'

'I think I'll stay. Rest a while.'

'No.' Zarlan-Jagr's voice quivered. 'Come now, Jesse. Lathqualla, morqwith.'

He opened the palm of his hand, spat into it, and clamped it shut. He spoke two more ancient wizard words: *brathqualla, jordqwith.* Wriggling the fingers of his other hand, Jesse didn't see the red-blue light arc across the cavern. Before it hit her, a gnarled and dripping claw shot out of the pool and deflected the wizard's magic.

'Jump now,' the voice from the pool ordered. A bent talon beckoned. 'Jump now. The wizard is trying to kill you.'

Jesse knew the voice was lying, yet she felt herself rising to her feet.

'Jump!'

Yes, Jesse thought without thinking – jump. Yes. Scared? No.

'No!' cried Zarlan and Iggywig.

The wizard issued a second arc of light.

The hand parried the wizard's magic like a shield deflecting a sword.

'Now! Jump!'

Jesse jumped.

The hand reached out to grab her.

Zarlan flew across to the pool, but he was too slow. Iggywig was quicker. From his hand he unleashed a Light Lock Charm. It covered the pool as if it were heavy duty cellophane covering a bowl of black jelly. Jesse rebounded backwards into Zarlan's outstretched arms.

'No,' the Drakmire screamed, shaking its claw.

'Yes,' Zarlan said, turning and carrying Jesse out of the cavern, toward the exit.

It was then that the Shadow Eaters arrived. Thousands of them crawled and scurried up the walls and ceiling like geckoes on hot sand.

'Run!' yelled Iggywig.

Jesse stumbled as Zarlan put her down. She swayed, feeling giddy and light-headed. What had happened?

'Run!' Iggywig urged again, already twenty yards ahead. 'Shadow Eaters!'

Jesse looked stupidly at Zarlan-Jagr.

'What's going on?'

Zarlan did not answer. He dragged her by the hand. 'This way,' he said. 'Don't look back.'

Jesse couldn't help herself. Both of their shadows were tall and thin, bowed around the walls and ceiling. Shadow Eaters were leaping and snarling, desperately trying to gain a grip on the ever-changing shadows.

She watched in disgust as her own shadow was torn away from the rocky wall. A hungry vast mouth opened wide to devour it. But as she turned towards the exit, the Shadow Eater lost its grip. A second Shadow Eater barged the first out of the way, howling. A third creature quickly seized the opportunity. It snatched Jesse's shadow. It held the head of her shadow up high like treasure, roaring with delight. As it snapped shut its jaws, the first Shadow Eater dived on top and they both tumbled in a heap on the ground, snarling and clawing at each other.

Jesse blundered towards the dark hole which led out of the caves, but she slipped, crashing to the hard rock floor just a few steps from freedom. The Shadow Eaters were quick. Howling, they descended on her, ripping at her shadow. She kicked two creatures away, but more came from the darkness and covered her like a biting mist.

'Ilalthatorg!'

Jesse glanced up to see Zarlan ablaze with white light, standing solid and defiant at the mouth of the cave. In his hands he held out a long staff, and from it poured fire and sparks and smoke. The Shadow Eaters screamed at the blinding light, cowered at the heat of fire and retreated into the darkness. But not before one of them tore a handful of shadow from Jesse's arm.

She yelled in pain, clutching her flesh and bone arm, and leapt to her feet. She staggered through the exit and out into the cold night air of inner city Caldazar. As she shape-shifted into a monster, one horror replaced another horror.

Eight

# Monster Rock Café

As they emerged onto the dimly lit streets of Caldazar, Jesse was glad she'd transformed into a monster. Zarlan had transformed, too, and by skilful illusion he'd somehow managed to change Iggywig into a grotesque giant. All around her she could see creatures like no others she had yet encountered in the Fairy Kingdoms. Here she saw unbelievable ugliness – three-eyed, one-legged, no-eared, hovering, bouncing, drooling, lumbering giants. The smallest was eight feet high, the tallest taller than a fully grown oak tree.

'Just act normally,' Zarlan-Jagr said.

'What does that mean?' Jesse spotted a few Caldazarian soldiers patrolling the alley. She rubbed her arm where her shadow had been. She tried to ignore the pain. 'I feel so awkward. Every time I walk the ground shakes. Every time I itch my head great lumps of scale and skin fly everywhere. I can't stop drooling slimy, thick green spit. How normal is that?'

'Totally,' Zarlan said. 'You're a natural. Now let's take a right at the end of this alley. That should be Graggsmunft Street and 5th.'

At the end of the alley Jesse turned into Graggsmunft Street. It reminded her of the madness of Piccadilly in London. Only here giant-bat-dragon-slug type creatures hustled and bustled with the indescribable and bizarre. A ten feet tall monster stopped and grunted at Jesse and caught hold of her shoulder.

'Hey, Macca. How yer doin, buddy?'

'Sorry. I'm not Macca,' Jesse said, shrugging his hand away from her shadow-less arm.

'Sure you are. Now where's that drink you promised?'

'No. You are mistaken.'

Jesse tried to walk around the monster, but he blocked her way.

'Not so fast, you good fer nothing cheapskate. You owe me a drink, Macca.'

Jesse couldn't think of anything to say. On the opposite side of the street she spied half a dozen Caldazarian soldiers.

'Well? Where are you going buddy?' The monster put his arm around Jesse's shoulders and guided her across the street. 'Monster Rock Café.'

Jesse looked up at the flashing red neon sign above the entrance. Even before she'd stepped inside, she could smell the stench of beer and spirits, cigarette smoke, and monster sweat.

'Disgusting,' she spluttered.

'I thought you'd like it,' the monster laughed, slapping Jesse's back.

Jesse glanced over her shoulder. The Caldazarian soldiers were busy stopping monsters and questioning them.

'Do as the big guy tells you,' Zarlan-Jagr said. 'He's a friend – our contact here in Caldazar. You lead and we'll follow you.'

Jesse nodded, feeling confused. Contact? Friend? He was certainly friendly. And she was startled by the size of the Monster Rock Café now that she was inside. At the far end, on a large stage, a band played loud music. There were six musicians in all – a drummer, a bass player, a trumpet player, two playing instruments that looked like but didn't sound like violins, and a singing mandolin player. Everywhere monsters were sitting at giant triangular tables, drinking and eating. A thick blue haze hovered above their heads. There wasn't much light – just a few muted wall torches.

At the bar, the monster who had called her Macca, lowered his voice and said: 'Just play along, Jesse. I'm Zarlan's friend.' He winked and slapped her back. 'So what'll it be, Macca?' he said loudly, pretending to be drunk; swaying from side to side.

'That's right, just play along,' Zarlan said, appearing at the bar with Iggywig. 'How goes it, friend?' He winked at the monster.

'As good as can be expected,' the monster said,

mysteriously. He winked back at Zarlan. 'So what'll it be?'

Jesse suddenly realised she didn't have a clue about alcohol. She'd tried it once at dad's birthday party while no one was looking – she'd spat it back into the glass. Revolting stuff!

Then another ghastly thought: she had no idea what monster drinks were called. 'Er ...'

'Targ,' the friendly monster said. 'Bar tender? We'll have two gallons of your best Targ – each.'

'Yes, Targ,' Jesse echoed, and tried to work out with growing alarm exactly what a gallon of Targ might look like. She didn't have to wait long.

'Cheers,' the friendly monster said, raising the enormous glass of purple and orange striped liquid to his lips. Then he lowered his voice and said seriously to Jesse: 'Don't drink a drop of it. Targ tastes like Caldazarian Dung Beetle droppings and just one sip will see you drunk for a fortnight.'

'You're joking,' Jesse said.

'I never joke about such things. Alcohol – especially a drink as strong as Targ – could have serious side effects.'

'What kind of side effects?'

'Terrible ones.'

'What do you mean by terrible?'

'You could be knocked unconscious, never to wake. Or you could die a slow painful death.'

'Would I bite dogs and cats?'

'What?'

'Oh, nothing,' Jesse said, smirking. She recalled what her mother had said about the malgrim fruit back on the outskirts of Loath Town. It seemed such a long time ago when they'd rested in that beautiful orchard.

'Besides,' the friendly monster carried on, downing the Targ and ordering another. 'You're not old enough to drink. Right? You're a kid.'

'Jesse be just a-kidding,' Iggywig said, gulping down more Targ.

'I'm eleven, almost,' she said, feeling confused. 'I think.'

'You think?'

'Fairy time is confusing. I didn't take Time Stopper potion the first time I came to the Fairy Kingdoms. I could be thirteen in human years.' She shrugged. 'I'm not sure.'

'I see. I feel as confused as you do.' He downed the Targ in one gulp. 'Or maybe the old Targ is hitting the spot.'

He banged the empty glass on the bar and the bar tender took it away for another refill.

'If you're ten, it's illegal for you to even be in here, let alone drink. But thirteen? That's all right. Caldazarians start drinking alcohol at twelve.'

'Twelve?' Jesse couldn't hide her shock. She held up the glass that was the size of a bucket. 'You can drink this stuff at twelve?'

'Great, isn't it?'

'No,' Jesse said, banging the glass down. Some of the liquid spilled over the rim and bubbled like paint stripper, eating away the bar. She noticed that the wooden surface was covered in holes and dips.

'Good stuff, eh?'

He tipped his head back and guzzled down his third Targ in one long gulp. He banged the empty glass down. 'Oh, and by the way, my name's Jasmire.'

The door crashed open and fifty or so Caldazarian soldiers stormed in, blocking all the exits. Their commander marched up onto the stage, knocked the singer out of the way and spoke into the microphone.

'Everyone stay in your seats. Do not move. We have Fairy Kingdom intruders amongst us. Sniff them out. Find them.'

Jesse shifted uncomfortably, even though she was monster. She watched as the drinkers mumbled into their glasses. No one moved to help the soldiers. No one, that was, until the commander spoke again.

'There is a price on the head of each fairy captured,' he announced.

'How much?' a monster called out for them all.

'One hundred thousand Heckles.'

The crowd stirred, whispered, nudged, laughed, muttered excitedly.

'One hundred thousand heckles for *each* fairy caught,' the commander added.

The Monster Rock Café erupted. Tables and chairs were shoved away, drinks went flying, and the monsters accused one another of being shape-shifting fairies.

'What did you say?' one said.

'You heard,' said another.

'No, don't think I did. Say it again.'

'You're a fairy.'

'Me? A fairy? No, you're the fairy. I always suspected you right from the first day we met!'

'Did you call me a fairy?'

'Yep, because that's what you are.'

'Why you good for nothing maggot! I'll give you fairy!'

'Come on then, if you think you are monster enough!'

A massive fight broke out. Chairs and tables and drinks flew through the air. Monsters were flattened by huge fists, some thrown against walls, other tossed like cabers across the room. It was mayhem.

'There's one!' a monster shouted, pointing in Jesse's direction.

A gang of monsters hurled themselves on top of a dopey-looking monster, who'd been rocking and rolling drunkenly beside Jesse on a bar stool. He was buried beneath a mountain of grappling monsters and pounding fists.

'This way,' Jasmire said, clenching Jesse's wrist.

She was yanked away from the brawlers and led toward the stage. The commander was still at the microphone, barking orders, telling his soldiers to stay firm at the exits.

The band did as all bands do when their audience decides to fight: they struck up and carried on playing as if nothing had happened. It was a fast urban monster beat.

'Stop that noise!' the commander ordered.

At the back of the café, the sound engineer slid the fader down on his mixing desk. The commander's voice disappeared, but he still shouted his orders though they couldn't be heard above the band and brawlers. Enraged, he threw the microphone onto the stage and kicked over the stand. Jesse thought he looked just like a rock star.

It was then that the real horror began.

The commander gave his soldiers a hand signal, and they started to fire into the crowd at random. A volley of eerie, silent Caldazarian gunfire flashed across Jesse's head. The drummer crashed to the ground, but the band continued playing without him.

'Get down,' Jasmire said, and they both hit the stage with a thump. Jesse suddenly realised that Zarlan and Iggywig were missing.

All the monsters stopped fighting and did the same. Some hid beneath upturned tables. Others crawled on hands and knees towards the exits. The Caldazarian soldiers held firm, still firing.

At that moment, the mandolin player crumpled in a heap. He did not move. A soldier knocked the sound engineer to one side and took control of the mixing desk. The commander picked up the microphone.

'Cease fire!'

The Monster Rock Café was silenced. A blue-green haze of cigarette and gun smoke hung in the humid air. Wounded monsters moaned.

'Fairies stand still. You are under arrest.'

Jesse watched in horror as the re-transformed Iggywig and Zarlan-Jagr were frog-marched out of the building, led by the gloating commander. What had happened to Zarlan's magic? And then she realised – it must have been the Targ. She felt helpless. She couldn't resist a sudden impulse to get up and help them. But she was wrestled to the ground by Jasmire.

'Don't be a fool,' he growled in her ear. 'What use are you if you're captured?'

'But my friends need my help.'

'Yes, but not now. It's not possible.'

'I could transform into a dragon and-'

'Get yourself captured, too.'

Jesse didn't have to think about Jasmire's words. Something else was happening.

'I'm changing,' she said.

'Can't you control it?'

'I'm trying, but it's no use.'

Jasmire stared at her angrily. 'You tried some Targ, didn't you?'

Jesse felt so ashamed. 'Yes,' she said lamely.

'I told you what would happen, didn't I?'

Jesse was close to tears. 'I can't control it. I'm changing.' Her body jerked. She could feel her hands and face transforming back into her fairy self. She gazed in fear at the café brimming with drunken monsters. 'Get me out of here.'

Together she and Jasmire hurtled through the doors and hurried in the opposite direction from the soldiers. They ran into the maze of darkened alleys, travelling further and deeper into the seedy quarter of Caldazar. Here no questions would be asked if a monster was seen with a fairy. For here, in the ghetto, the population had more pressing concerns: which monster or fairy would become the next fresh meal.

Nine

# The Winged Demon

They reached Jasmire's back street flat in the dead of the never-ending night. An unseen creature snarled three times close by in the deep dark shadows. Flat echoing footfalls came and went in alleys nearby, but Jesse saw no one. She was glad. She didn't *want* to see anyone. The thought of monsters on the loose, stalking their next meal in the dark scared her. She'd had enough of monsters for one day. She shuddered.

'Mind the boxes,' Jasmire said, stepping over piles of rubbish in the hallway.

Something squelched disgustingly beneath Jesse's foot. What had she trodden in? She dare not look. Ahead she could see the debris-strewn living quarters of Jasmire. What a disappointment. What a mess!

'You really live like this?' Jesse said without thinking.

'Its not so bad, once you get used to it.' Jasmire bolted the door.

Jesse shook her head. In the far corner of the living-room she could see twenty cased instruments – cellos maybe. Bunged on top of them were sweet wrappers, mouldy yoghurt pots, stinking empty milk cartons, bits of half eaten food, such as cheese and carrots, raw cabbage and spaghetti. Closer, she saw discarded pizza boxes, silver take-away food containers, and thousands of curled and ripped sheets of music. Thousands and thousands of maggots oozed amongst the rubbish.

'This is disgusting,' she said. 'How can you live like this?'

'As I said, it's not too bad once you get used to it.'

Jasmire scooped up a mug full of maggots from the floor and began to devour them – in great gulps as if drinking coffee.

'What! ... What are you doing?' Jesse said, appalled. She felt her stomach turn.

'Snack time,' Jasmire smiled, swigging back another mouthful. He held out his empty mug. 'Here. Take a scoop full. Help yourself. They're delicious.'

'Sick!'

'Suit yourself. These are home-grown organic maggots. Not the factory-farmed rubbish a supermarket might sell. Are you sure you wouldn't like some? They're mighty juicy.'

'No way.'

Jesse felt bile rising in her throat and

swallowed it back down.

'Sorry, but it's the best I can offer.'

'Then I'll eat nothing,' she said indignantly. She yawned and stretched. 'I'm beat. Do you have anywhere I can sleep without getting eaten alive by those things you're munching?'

'The old guest room is quite clean,' Jasmire said. 'It hasn't been slept in for years. Come on. I'll show you to your room.'

Jasmire carried Jesse up three flights of giant stairs. Each step was taller than her. At last, they reached the attic room. Jasmire opened the door, put her down, and ushered her in. The semi-darkened room smelled of something unsavoury, so Jesse tried to put it out of her mind. Even in the half-light she could make out giant cobwebs sprawled corner to corner.

Jasmire spoke some words that Jesse didn't understand. A green haze lit up the room. It seemed to come from everywhere.

'Too clean, for my liking,' Jasmire groaned. 'Still, as the old human folk say: beggars can't be choosers, now can they?'

He laughed and said goodnight, closing the door behind him.

'Goodnight, and thanks,' Jesse said.

'Sweet dreams,' Jasmire replied, his voice fading as he descended the giant stairs. 'Oh, by the way, if you hear shouting and bawling in the night, don't let it bother you.'

'Er ... okay,' Jesse said uneasily. 'What might it be?'

'Drunken monsters staggering out of the *Ole Red-Eyed Dragon* pub most likely. Or it could be smugglers, drunken no doubt, fixing deals in the alley below. Or maybe ...'

'Thanks,' Jesse cut in. 'I think I get the picture.'

'Sleep well.'

'I will,' she said, knowing only too well that she would stay wide-eyed most of the night, worrying.

She looked up at the huge shutters that hid a giant window. It was no use – she needed to shape-shift if she were to see out. She transformed into her monster self and opened the shutters, staring out over Caldazar. In a bizarre kind of way, what she saw had its own strange beauty. Silhouetted against the inky sky, she could see the twin spires. To the west, densely packed jagged teeth-like buildings dominated the skyline. There were sparkling lights, and behind the lights monster shadows went about their night-time business.

When Jasmire's footfalls had faded completely, Jesse traced her finger through an inch of dust that carpeted the giant window ledge. Mum would have a fit if she saw this, she thought, grinning. Although there were no maggots crawling about on the floor, it was far from clean.

Jesse remained still and silent for a long time, simply watching. The air was chilled. A wolf-like creature howled close by. Bats flew like mini stealth planes, victory rolling, fast, silent, scarcely glimpsed. Then gone. For a moment she felt terribly homesick and alone. Mum and Dad had taken her to many air shows. It was their annual pilgrimage in the long, hot summer holidays. The first time she saw a Stealth Bomber at Mildenhall she'd thought it must be a spacecraft from the film *Star Wars*.

'I miss you, Mum and Dad,' she whispered, and wiped a tear from her eye.

She watched the moons' light reflected as though radiant silver eyes. High clouds seemed fused to the heavens – trampolines for the stars that never jumped. Then there was the stark silhouette of Caldazar itself – sharp, pointed, hard, jagged like monster-made fangs.

There was a knock at the door.

Jesse jumped, flushed with adrenalin, heart pounding, eyes wide.

'It's only me,' Jasmire said. 'May I come in? I've managed to get you something you might like to eat and drink.'

'Yes. Come in,' Jesse replied, turning back to the Caldazarian skyline. She transformed with ease back into her fairy self. She didn't want him to see her monster self, for although the Targ's effects had worn off, her shame and embarrassment had not.

Jasmire placed a tray of food and drink on the end of Jesse's bed.

'Beautifully cruel, isn't it?' he said, pointing to Caldazar.

'Yes,' she said. 'Tonight is filled with sadness and hope.'

'Explain, please.'

'My friends are out there somewhere. That's worrying. But there's hope once we begin our search for them.'

Jasmire's face crumpled, mouth turned down like a segment of orange.

'It's too dangerous, Jesse. Your shape-shifting is unpredictable.'

'The Targ has worn off. I'm sure I can hold any shape I want for as long as I want.' She touched the Seeing-Stone in her pocket absently.

'I disagree. I think it's too risky. If you reveal your fairy self to the creatures here you will be ...'

Jesse needed no explanation. She understood the peril. Still, what was worse? Hanging around doing nothing, or taking a chance to find her friends?

'Anyone of them would have come looking for me if I were in their position,' she said.

'You have good, loyal friends, but I think they want you to be safe.'

'Yes, I'm sure they do. But they need my help. I'm free, they're not.'

Jesse fixed Jasmire a warm stare.

'Will you help me?'

Jasmire shook his head slowly. 'I'm sorry, Jesse. I think it is too risky. You are being hunted all over Caldazar. What would be the point? Your shape-shifting skills are not stable enough. You'd be captured in no time – killed. And I'd be sent to the Harjakan Salt Mines to smash rock-salt twenty six hours a day.'

Jesse said nothing as he left the room. She had for a moment considered revealing her Seeing-Stone to him, her gift of awesome magic from the

Elders of Elriad. But she'd thought better of it. She had nothing to prove to Jasmire. If he wouldn't help her, she'd come up with her own plan.

*

After she had eaten with relish the food provided by Jasmire, Jesse climbed into the giant bed. She was glad that there were no mirrors in the room. The thought of watching her reflection in the spooky green half-light crammed her with trepidation. Best not to think too much about the events since arriving in Caldazar, she told herself. Try to sleep. But it was difficult. She thought about her friends, imprisoned somewhere, or worse. She tossed and turned, thinking about what she could do to help them. Ideas and plans came and went as she drifted in and out of sleep. She knew she would remember none of them when she woke again. Besides, there were no plans worth remembering. It was all her fault. She was the one the monsters were searching for. She was ...

When sleep claimed her, she dreamed she could fly and shape-shift with complete mastery. She and her mother and Perigold were eagles, high and free, gliding on the air currents above the Knoll of Knowing in the good Kingdom of Troth.

It was a beautiful dream, while it lasted.

*

Jesse was woken by a brilliant blue burst of light in the middle of the night. Thunder cracked and shook plaster dust from the ceiling down onto the dirty blanket that Jesse now clung to. Through the grimy window, from the giant bed in which she found herself, she could see huge creatures gathered in huddles out on the narrow wind-blown alley. They were peering skyward.

She sat up to take a better look around the drab room. The green hazy light Jasmire had commanded by voice alone was out. The room was huge and lit by a single candle which flickered on a table in the far corner. Had they been there before she'd slept? There was no other furniture. The floor was as bare as the walls. Another flash of lightning illuminated the room. This time she saw a round mirror fixed to the opposite wall. Had it been there before? No! What was going on?

A face appeared in the mirror for a fleeting second and then vanished.

'Who's there?' Jesse said.

A jagged fork of purple lightning flashed. Another crack of thunder shook the bed. More lightning quickly followed.

Jesse drew in a sharp breath.

The creatures in the alley outside cheered.

Something scuttled across the wooden floor and stopped beneath her bed.

Jesse instinctively drew up her knees and hugged them. 'Who's there?'

Darkness, but for the dim flicker of the candle. Ghostly shadows danced on the walls. A fourth flash of lightning lit up the room for a moment.

Jesse screamed. Another face in the mirror leaned out into the room. It disappeared. The face had been green and grotesque. Dark glaring eyes and holes where a nose should have been.

Something scuttled across the floorboards in the gloom and stopped beneath her bed.

More cheering rose and fell from the growing crowd of monsters outside.

Where am I? Jesse wondered amidst her fear.

'Welcome to Caldazar, my pretty,' said a familiar voice.

'Dendrith?'

'Don't just sit there trembling, you pathetic little brat,' Dendrith scolded. 'Pick us up and get us out of here. Monsters hate witches almost as much as they hate fairies. Move!'

Jesse scanned the room. There on the table next to the candle she could see the glass egg, containing the vile witch sisters. Now that most definitely hadn't been there before the last strike of lightning.

'Hurry,' said Gwendrith, pressing her gruesome face against the glass. 'Before it's too late. Hurry. NOW!'

Jesse jumped out of bed and grabbed the egg. For a moment she froze in the semi-darkness. More lightning and thunder. Another face popped out of the mirror and vanished. The scuttlers beneath the bed revealed themselves. Darting red eyes, hairy, multi-legged creatures about the size of rats were huddled together near one bed leg. They snarled, showing silver biting teeth.

'Run!' Dendrith urged.

Jesse needed no second bidding. She sprouted wings on her back and flew as fast as they would carry her to the door. She yanked the handle. It was locked. Again and again and again she tugged, but it wouldn't open.

'It's locked,' she said.

'Of course it's locked, you stupid brat. You are a prisoner here. Climb out of the window,' Gwendrith ordered.

'And whatever you do, do not look in that mirror,' Dendrith added. 'You've seen what lurks there. Do not become another victim.'

The scuttlers moved swiftly from under the bed toward her, gnashing and hissing and spitting. Talons lurched out and grabbed empty space.

Jesse leapt over them and flew up to the open window. She began to haul herself out onto the balcony, but she ... twisted her ... head ... and glanced in the mirror.

'NO!' she howled. 'No, no, NO!'

*

Screaming madly, Jesse wrenched her eyes from the outlandish reflections. Another nightmare took its place: Zundrith's demons swarmed around her. Millions of tiny creatures descended through the open window. She was swamped in seconds, fell backwards into the room and cracked her head hard on the floor. The glass egg tumbled from her hand and hit the floor with a thump. The scuttlers seized the moment. But they were no match for Zundrith's demons. Screams and squeals filled the room. Talons swiped and teeth gnashed. Darkness and fur fought wildly, snarled, clawed, and howled.

The battle was over a minute later. Feeling groggy, Jesse was helped by an invisible force to her feet. She was surrounded by a cloud of darkness. Whispers foul and foreign attacked her ears. She clamped her hands over them but couldn't shut out their incessant bedlam.

Then she saw it – a winged demon somewhat bigger than the rest. It penetrated the dark and hovered before her eyes.

'What do you want?' Jesse slurred. She felt dizzy in its presence.

'You,' it snarled. 'Do not resist.'

Jesse eased back slowly.

'You think I'll go with you quietly?' she laughed, trying to mask her fear. 'Never. I'll fight you with every bone in my body.'

'I doubt it,' Dendrith said.

Jesse glanced to her left. There on the floor was the glass egg, jammed against the skirting board. It was cracked badly but both witches were still trapped inside.

'The High Witch, Zundrith, sent them to do her bidding,' Dendrith said. 'It's over, Jameson. Smash the egg now and free us. We'll be merciful. We promise, don't we, Gwendrith?'

'Oh yes, cross our black hearts and hope to die.'

Dendrith cackled. 'You crack me up, dear sister. You are so funny.'

'Why thank you, dearest sister. I know I am.'

Dendrith narrowed her smouldering eyes.

'Well ... Jesse Jameson, what will it be? Mercy? Or something foul and wicked and horribly unpleasant?'

'I'll never help you two. Never!'

'Unpleasant then?' Gwendrith sniggered. 'Oh good. I was praying that the little sooth-saying brat was going to make that choice. Kids and brains just don't go together. I love doing unpleasant.'

'I know you do, dear dearest sister. It won't be long now before we are free. Zundrith will see to that.'

The winged demon hissed and grew instantly to Jesse's size.

Jesse gasped and backed away gradually.

'Zundrith?' Dendrith quizzed. 'Is it really you, Sister in Suffering?'

'Yes, it is,' said Gwendrith, rubbing her hands together excitedly. 'It is. It is! IT IS!'

'Praise to all that is evil and vile,' Dendrith sang. 'Free us, my queen. Free us so that we may join you in your glorious revenge.'

The winged demon hissed at them and spat a golf-sized ball of red phlegm. It completely covered the egg. The witches were silent.

'I am not Zundrith,' the winged demon growled deeply. 'I have no name. I serve only my mistress. All of our fates are in her blessed hands.' It signalled with a nod and the red egg jerked into the air and floated out of the window, carried by a dark cloud up and beyond the never-ending Caldazarian night. It imploded into another dimension as it reached the twin spires which continued to drain the stars and moons of their light.

'Gone,' the winged demon said. 'I hope my mistress punishes them.'

'For what?' Jesse said, trying desperately to stall for time, so that she could think of a way out of the mess she was in.

'She will punish them for their stupidity.'

'Er ... because they got caught, you mean?' Think Jesse Jameson. Think!

'Yes. Only fools allow themselves to die and get imprisoned in a glass egg. How stupid.'

'I agree,' Jesse said. She felt the Seeing-Stone in her pocket but was unsure of what to do with its power. 'But in fairness to them, they were up against masters of magic. Do you know of Iggywig and Zarlan-Jagr?'

'No,' said the winged demon. 'But they will soon know of me, my mistress, and her dark army of followers.'

'They already do,' said a voice from the shadows.

The demon twisted around awkwardly to glimpse the blow that hit it between the eyes. It crashed to the ground and twitched. It was unconscious.

Stepping out of the shadows, Jesse saw Jasmire.

'I changed my mind,' he said, a warm monster smile igniting his face.

'Thanks,' Jesse said. She peered down at the motionless winged demon. 'Thanks for everything.'

'And I have a secret to tell,' Jasmire admitted.

Jesse could see from the shine in his eye that what was about to come would be a revelation. Without warning she was sucked into a vision. She stood beside the sleeping Perigold, his face webbed and crawling with centi-spiders. She glanced around the chamber. Five slabs were empty – just the same as before. There were eight motionless members of the Union of Thirteen. Her eyes rested on one of the empty slabs. It read Geo-Staibbe *descended* and she shuddered.

The name plate glowed a dull red and the letters began to rearrange themselves. There were two new words now, created from Geo-Stabbie ... *Bogie Beast.*

Jesse lurched, gasped, grasped the cold stone corner of the slab on which Perigold slept.

'Bogie Beast,' she muttered. 'A member of the Union of Thirteen?'

The chamber swam in and out of view. Her legs gave way and she gripped the slab harder. Then her eyes fell upon the empty slab with Zarlan-Jagr's name plate on it. She began to feel calmer – she could hear the wizard's voice in her head. His sing-song melody soothed her. 'A good friend of mine,' she whispered. 'Out there somewhere. I must help him and the others. We need to find the New Master of Darkness. We need to find a counter charm to wake Perigold.'

'Yes,' said Jasmire. 'We do.'

Jesse was confused. Jasmire? In her vision? She looked at the remaining empty slab and read the name plate: Trondian-Yor *missing.*

'Not anymore,' said Jasmire, and Jesse slipped as if on ice from her vision. The chamber was sucked like water down a plughole.

'You?'

'Yes,' Jasmire said. His grotesque monster face and body morphed in seconds into a tall, slender quargkin. He was dressed in a deep purple, flowing cloak, golden shirt, and white trousers. His boots were a florescent orange – tipped at the toe with a lick of black.

He is so handsome, Jesse thought, like a pop idol or Hollywood star.

'Trondian-Yor,' he said, his voice changed now out of all recognition. Gone were the gravel tones of Jasmire, replaced by a melodic voice even sweeter and more soothing than Zarlan's voice.

'I would love to answer your questions,' Trondian-Yor said, raising an open palm towards her. 'But what do you prefer? A nice cosy chat about how I came to be here, pretending to be Jasmire? My history as a member of the Union of Thirteen? Or should we hunt down the scum who've got your friends locked up?'

'We talk on the way to the Prison Chamber.'

Trondian-Yor laughed. 'You never give up, do you, Jesse Jameson?'

Ten

# Stinkburrow

Stepping over the winged demon, they hurried out into the teeming monster-riddled streets of never-ending night time Caldazar.

The maze of narrow filthy alley ways was dark and foggy. As Jesse followed Trondian-Yor she glanced over her shoulder. The echoing footfalls seemed to come from all directions. Monsters huddled in shady doorways striking deals, Heckles exchanged for small packets. Red and green eyes glowed menacingly from misty corners, and unseen lurkers growled, snarled and hissed.

As they hurried through the fog, Trondian-Yor spoke little, but what he told was incredible and mysterious. He informed Jesse he was the youngest member of the Union of Thirteen – some one hundred years or so younger than Perigold in human time. He'd been trained by Zarlan. He called himself prentice to the wizard who had once studied with the Elders of Elriad on their hidden Island of Wisblakria surrounded by sea mist, sea monsters and magic. But he could not speak about it. He had been sworn to secrecy – a vital part of a white wizard's code. The code of conduct meant that all of the Thirteen agreed to a set of rules – ways to behave, standards of acting that reminded Jesse all too much of Mrs Wobble's class rules.

As they turned into a courtyard, flanked by tall, jagged red buildings that look as if they are about to topple or collapse, Jesse asked: 'Why were you in disguise as Jasmire?'

'My life is in as much danger as yours,' he said mysteriously. 'We are hunted. We are all that stands in the way of this kingdom being taken over by the dark forces of the New Master of Darkness.'

'What is this New Master of Darkness?'

'He is part Drith and part Don. The Driths are as you know evil witches and warlocks, a race of selfish, hurtful fairy folk, and the Dons once had great power in the Naargapire. They ruled the vampire lands of the Naargapire like lords and kept the ordinary folk in slavery. But they were driven into hiding during the Sixth Caldazarian War.'

Jesse nodded her understanding.

'The Skaardrithadon, as he is known to his people, is a mysterious creature. And he also has a titanic taste for blood.'

'A vampire?'

Trondian-Yor nodded, Jesse shuddered. A chilling breeze whipped up around their legs and was gone.

'Have you met him?' Jesse said.

'Once.'

'What did he look like?'

'I didn't see his face, just the filthy evil presence that clings to him like a lightless cloud of darkness.'

Trondian-Yor stopped outside a building with a large, battered metal door. He looked at Jesse.

'I have it on good authority that once you step into his cloud of darkness your mind is instantly wiped of all memory, purged of every good thought and filled with dark, evil, selfish, greedy thoughts that send all but the strongest insane and delirious. All non-monsters are transformed forever into hideous things – wandering, waiting for his call to do his bidding.'

'Sounds awful.'

'It is,' Trondian-Yor said, waving his hand in a sideways figure of eight. The metal door whooshed up. 'My sister is living proof. She entered his cloud a calm, sane young white witch ... and left a screaming, demented mad woman, who now wanders the streets of Caldazar swearing, spitting and cursing everyone she meets.'

'That's terrible,' Jesse said, shaking her head. Trondian-Yor said nothing. He didn't need to. He could keep secret many things, but his anger and pain were plain to see.

'Not another word,' he commanded, as they entered the building. The door swished shut.

He led her through halls and corridors to an open-plan courtyard deep inside the building. The floor was paved with stone mosaics of black and gold repeating patterns. A small dragon's head fountain squirted a high arc of water into a rippling round pond. She could feel the magic in the air, the invisible presence of charm and spell. Her heart thumped in her temples and she rubbed her ache absently.

Trondian broke the silence, making her jump with his words. 'Recognise this?' He opened his palm to reveal a small obsidian Seeing-Stone.

'Yes,' Jesse said. 'Zarlan gave it to me at Talonscar.' She felt her empty pocket. 'How did you get it?'

'Magic.' He smiled. 'Don't worry, I didn't steal it. It came to me of its own free will.'

'How?'

'How else?'

'Magic,' they said together, laughing.

Jesse noticed he had the most wonderful smiling eyes. She felt happy in his company.

'What does it do?'

'Many things, I think. I do not know for sure. But it helped me to see into other dimensions, and I think it might help me see people's auras.'

'And?'

'Er ...' Jesse racked her memory. 'Nothing else.'

'It saved the biggest part of your natural magic – stored it so that it could be used again when the time was right.'

'The biggest part?'

'Magic you have yet to use, yet to discover deep inside.'

'Inside where, the Seeing-Stone?'

'Yes, but it's also inside your mind. That's where the real magic hides. It's like a vast warehouse of possibilities. When you need magic most, when your back is against the wall, and there seems to be no way out – then you will know what I mean.'

'How will I know?'

'Believe me, you just will. You are full of wonders, full of enchantment and spell-making. You are full of great good. Believe in yourself, Jesse Jameson. When no one else around you believes in your magic, believe in yourself.'

Jesse nodded. In that moment, something unsaid reached out from the wizard's mind and held her. That something was more meaningful than words, more touching than music, some invisible force greater than love. Years later, when she'd passed through the Dark Walled Veil of Knowing; when Trondian-Yor had left her forever to pass into the Deeper Realms of Elriad, she'd return to this moment in her mind and treasure it.

He handed the obsidian to her. 'Place it on your third eye in the middle of your forehead and close your other eyes.'

Jesse put the obsidian against her forehead. It felt icy cold. Instantly the room changed. The two pillars in the corner of the room vibrated with the same kind of energy she'd seen at the Portal of Talonscar. Between them emerged a mass of swirling energy like a light-filled cyclone. In its centre – an eye of calm. The eye winked.

'Come on,' Trondian-Yor said, grabbing Jesse's hand.

It was like stepping into a revolving door, and emerging not from the street to a hotel foyer, but from a sparse room into a snake pit. The pit was a giant half dome turned upside down.

'Where are we?' she said, looking around.

'I cannot say,' Trondian-Yor said. He motioned to the rim of the dome. 'But beyond this bowl, along the flats and plains of this place is ...'

His voice trailed away like steam from an old train's chimney.

'What's wrong?' Jesse said, her voice lifting an octave.

'We're being followed. Someone else has just slipped through the Portal. Listen.'

Jesse strained her ears. She heard nothing but a deep hum, coming from beyond the rim. She glanced over her shoulder and slowly scanned the dome. There seemed to be no way in or out.

'I don't hear or see anyone,' she said.

'They're here.'

'They?'

'Yes – there's two of them. They are camouflaged.'

'Chameleon Sweets?'

'Perhaps. But most likely a Chamo Charm.'

'What should we do?'

Jesse scanned around the dome again, but couldn't see the intruders.

'I think it's time for us to shape-shift,' Trondian-Yor urged.

Jesse did as the young wizard told her. He sounded anxious, which worried her. Light spilled into her mind as she visualised her new transformation. The flux between changing bones, blood and flesh melted then stiffened. It felt good to be a dragon again. She launched herself into the air, wings flapping huge steady beats.

'Follow me,' Trondian-Yor said, transforming into a Baalvosh.

'You look disgusting,' Jesse said.

'Thanks,' said Trondian-Yor, winking at her.

She was glad she was a red dragon. He couldn't see her blushes.

*

High above the bowl Jesse could see hundreds more bowls stretching for miles across the landscape. It was a stark, grey world. There were no trees or buildings – just huge bowls that looked like machined craters. In between them the terrain was smooth and flat and featureless.

'Where are we?' Jesse said.

'Stinkburrow,' Trondian-Yor said.

'Stinkburrow?' Jesse's smile soon faded.

'Beneath each bowl is a prison chamber. All of the Caldazarian's enemies are imprisoned here. Well, the ones captured. Any non-monster is immediately arrested and imprisoned without a trial. They are all guilty of one simple crime: they are different; non-monsters.'

'Why do the Caldazarian's fear non-monsters?'

'It goes way back in time – long before the Spriggan Wars and around the time of the last

Great Unbalancing seven thousand years ago, when the human kingdom was invaded by the Dark Trolls and Flying Dragons that once ruled Finnigull.'

'Yes, Perigold once told me about it. It was an age when humans were slaves to the Dark Trolls in the Northern Hemisphere, and slaves to the Flying Dragons in the South. Magic, charms, potions, visions and shape-shifting were everyday normal things. Eventually, after a thousand year war the humans won.'

'Very good history lesson. You listened well.' He nodded his approval. 'But Perigold forgot to mention the monsters and the fairy people, and the awful time of the Vampire-Fairy wars, didn't he?'

'What about them?' Jesse said, intrigued.

'The human and the ruling fairy wizards joined forces near the end of the war. They agreed to create the monsters to help them win against the trolls and dragons.'

'What – all monsters?'

'Yes, all monsters. Just like Frankenstein's monster, I suppose. And once they had won the war, they no longer needed the monsters or the vampires who'd lent their support on and off. They sent the vampires back to their homeland, the Naargapire, and tried to forget they existed. That suited the vampires, who had little time for the affairs of humans after such a betrayal, but they did have a taste for human blood. They grudgingly gave the monsters Caldazar as a homeland, and began the myths about the place and its inhabitants. The human and fairy wizards kept the bad monster myth going for years.'

'Why?'

'Some say because they feared the monsters. Which makes sense. They'd seen them in battle. They were awesome warriors. And they no longer wanted to take responsibility for them, so it was easier to contain them in Caldazar. Lock them up in their own city, in a far away fairy kingdom, and forget they ever existed. After all, perhaps one day the monsters might turn on the wizards who'd created them.'

'That's awful.'

'Yes, it is. So you now see why non-monsters are deeply mistrusted.'

'I can see why,' Jesse said. 'But should all the bad things that happened years ago give the Caldazarians the right to imprison non-monsters now?'

'The Caldazarians would say – yes,' Trondian-Yor said. 'A few years ago, a few humans and fairies began to trade in exotic spices on the borders of Caldazar. It seemed that thousands of years of mistrust had at last started to be repaired. But it didn't quite work out, and things got out of hand. People got greedy, started to bend the unspoken rules to make more money. Humans and fairies were once again mistrusted and imprisoned. It was the monsters' turn to act out of fear and hatred.'

'And you? What do you think to the creatures which are imprisoned?'

'What I think is not important. I speak as a

member of the Union. There is your answer.'

Yes, Jesse thought, it was a stupid question. It was clear that Trondian-Yor was against the Caldazarian's imprisonment of non-monsters. Why else would he be helping her? Suddenly a shocking thought erupted in her mind. Unless he really was Jasmire – a Caldazarian monster – and this was a trap. But that was a silly idea. Hadn't he helped her escape the Caldazarians? Given her refuge in his filthy flat? Rescued her from the winged demon!

Trondian-Yor smiled and nodded.

Jesse followed his gaze. Below was another gigantic bowl. Someone was standing on the rim, waving a light.

'Now the fun begins,' the quargkin wizard said. 'We will free our friends and allies.'

Jesse felt her three hearts beating like the African drum music her Dad loved so much. Her thoughts wandered homeward for a moment. In her mind's eye, she saw mum and dad dancing frantically to the beat, giggling, swinging each other around and around. She joined them and squealed with delight.

Snapped from her memories, they flew down quickly. Jesse transformed into her fairy self.

'Welcome to Stinkburrow,' the monster before her said without a hint of laughter in his eyes. Trondian-Yor and the monster embraced. 'Although I wouldn't welcome my worst enemy to this non-monster hell-hole.'

'This is Androst,' said the young wizard. 'He has been a great assistance to the Union of

Thirteen in Caldazarian territories for many years.'

'A pleasure,' Androst said, blushing. 'But me? Great? I think not.'

'Why do you help the Union?' Jesse asked without thinking.

Trondian-Yor glanced sharply at Jesse.

'It's okay,' Androst said, smiling. He had two enormous black, pear-shaped eyes and two vertical slots for nose holes. Both eyes and nose holes widened. 'She has a right to know if she can trust me or not. I find children have a way of getting to the truth without mixing words.'

Trondian-Yor nodded, obviously pleased that Androst had taken no offence.

'When I was a young monster, my whole family were thrown into these prison chambers without trial.'

'What did they do?'

'It's what they didn't do that got them imprisoned. They didn't agree with the Caldazarian idea of imprisoning non-monsters. They believed that they should be allowed to choose their own friends and business partners. You see, my mother and father were traders in exotic Caldazarian spices. They traded with a few non-monsters from Finnigull and Troth and supplied them illegally to many high-ranking officials. Even – to the President, Generals, and senior Government ministers. Mum told me that everything was fine – until one day they sold non-monster spices to another trader who started to supply his own business colleagues. Soon the non-monster spices were more popular with the common monster than anything Caldazar could offer.'

'Why was that so bad?' Jesse said.

'Because it snowballed.' Androst shook his head. 'The common monster wanted more than Finnigullian spices. They thought they should be allowed to trade in any type of goods – foods, clothes, livestock. Before long there was chaos along the Caldazarian borders. All the Spiral Gates were closed. No one was allowed in and no Caldazarian was allowed out.'

'Are your family still imprisoned here?' Jesse motioned to the hole in the ground, where she could just see the dull shine of a ladder.

'No,' Androst said. 'I am the only one who survived. I was just a small child, barely able to recall those sad days, when my family were arrested. They were quickly 'disappeared' without a trace. No one has heard or seen them for over forty years.'

'So why didn't they 'disappear' you?'

'I am what the President calls *a reminder to all monsters of my family's betrayal.* Ironically they made me Chief Prison Warden of the Non-Monster Prison Chambers.' He gave out a hollow laugh. 'I am responsible for keeping all non-monsters locked up. The President knows that one day I'll try to help the non-monsters escape. That's why he keeps so many cameras watching my every move. It keeps him amused.'

Androst led the way down the ladder into the Prison Chamber. At every turn there were cameras

– tiny eye-like machines fixed to the walls. It was a dimly lit place, made from the same smooth grey material as the bowl above them.

Thousands of enormous prison cells lined the corridors and Jesse heard the moans and groans of non-monsters echoing in her ears. It was a horrid sound and briefly reminded Jesse of her own mother's imprisonment in Dendrith's Dungeons.

'I know this might be a stupid question,' she said. 'But won't those cameras be filming us and sending the President all the evidence he needs?'

Androst smiled, stopping at cell b72943. 'No,' he said. 'I've been er ... how should I say ... tinkering with the film sent to the President's office for three months now. I've rigged the cameras so his officials in the Presidential Palace only see what I want them to see – old footage.

'I've released most of the non-monsters over the past month. They are now safely with their families in Troth, Finnigull and beyond. Some even as far as the Naargapire.'

He opened the door of cell b72943. It had once been a maze of single cells which had been knocked into one massive hangar-like structure.

'This is not a prison anymore, Jesse Jameson,' he said, 'but a command centre for the Non-Monster Alliance. In six hours and forty two minutes, we go to war.'

The sight which greeted Jesse was impressive. Beyond Iggywig, Zarlan, Kumo, Jake and the Dragon Hunter, tens of thousands of Talonscarians and fairy folk filled a massive chamber. They looked after their flying beasts, cleaned weapons, and prepared for the battle to come. Jesse saw all kinds of fairy folk – Nuggies, Portunes, Spriggans, Yarthkins, Corrigans, even Goblins and Trolls. It was a marvellous sight – fairy folk working together.

'When did you get here?' Jesse asked her companions.

'An hour ago,' said Zarlan. 'Although Kumo, Jake, and the Dragon Hunter have been here a while longer.'

'What's going on?' Jesse said, feeling her chest tighten.

'It's complicated,' Kumo Diaz said. 'That's why I'm leaving. I want nothing to do with ... with this ... war of yours. I'm a simple tracker. I have done my job. Now I leave.'

'Yes,' the Dragon Hunter agreed. 'You have tricked us Zarlan-Jagr. We came here to find the Skaardrithadon, to find a cure for Perigold's sleep.' He motioned to the enormous army behind him. 'This has nothing to do with us. And Jesse and Jake are just children. War is not their concern.'

*

Zundrith clasped the glass egg in her claw and studied it. Gathered around her were her demons – insubstantial, dark shadows. Their whispers and mumblings of discontent hummed like a swarm of angry bees.

'It's time, my wretched little retinue, to unite with the Skaardrithadon,' Zundrith said. She spat on the egg and launched it like a bowling ball down into the frozen river. It smashed against a tooth of ice and shattered into two clean halves. Great plumes of black and red smoke poured like a chimney fire. The witch-sisters, Dendrith and Gwendrith, stepped out from the smoke. They were no longer tiny but had returned to their normal size. They strode, like the antithesis of glamour models on a catwalk, with purpose and confidence – transparent ghosts hell-bent on revenge.

'Where should we go to meet with the Skaardrithadon?' Dendrith said.

'You meet at the Point of Darkness beneath the twin spires in three hours. Take my forces with you and destroy all who stand in your way. Make the Talonscarian creatures suffer for their treachery.'

'It will be my pleasure, mistress,' Dendrith said.

'Yes,' echoed Gwendrith. 'The pleasure is all ours.' A few wasps spewed from her mouth.

'Go, then, my Sisters in Suffering, and complete our revenge. I have craved it ever since Jagr's magic locked me in this hell.'

'And I shall kill that wizard as he killed me,' Dendrith said. 'Our suffering shall be revenged, sisters.'

'And that brat, Jesse Jameson? What shall we do with her?' Gwendrith asked.

'She is a sister,' Zundrith said. 'She is young. Capture her and bring her to me. We will exchange her golden glow for something a little more sinister. She can still be trained in the Weird Dark Sciences of Witchcraft.'

'Are you sure we wouldn't be better off without her?' Gwendrith said. 'Zarlan-Jagr's influence on her mind shouldn't be under-estimated. She has the blessing of the Elders of Elriad.'

'If she fails my training, or resists my will,' Zundrith said, 'she will die anyway.'

'How?'

'I will kill her.'

*

'This war is everyone's concern,' Zarlan said. 'You are making decisions without all of the facts.'

'What facts do I need to know?' Kumo said. 'Wars kill thousands. That is a fact that I want no part of.'

'If we do not fight the Skaardrithadon and his army of evil, then millions will die. Millions of Talonscarians and millions of fairy folk.'

'How do we know that this is not a plot created by you and the Union of Thirteen?' the Dragon Hunter said. 'You seem to have your own agenda.'

'It is not a plot.' Zarlan's eyes saddened. 'I am an honourable member of the Thirteen. I am sworn to protect the good and the innocent, to fight evil, and fight-'

'Spare me a sermon,' Kumo Diaz said. 'I'm leaving.'

Jesse watched Kumo Diaz as he strolled out of Cell b72943. He slammed the door shut hard.

'Come on,' the Dragon Hunter said. 'We leave, too.'

Jesse knocked the Dragon Hunter's hand away. 'I need to hear the whole story. Then I will decide if I want to stay or not.'

'Iggywig be a-willing to hear the story, as welling.'

'Me, too,' said Jake.

'But you and Jesse are just children. What do you know about war? War kills. This war will kill many - like all wars.'

'Please let me explain,' Zarlan said. He wriggled the finger of his left ringless hand. A flash of pink-blue light arched onto the floor from his finger tips. A table and chairs appeared, filled with food and drink.

'Let us talk.'

'Yes, pleasing.' Iggywig sipped a purple liquid from a tall thin glass.

'As I said earlier, this war concerns everyone. The Skaardrithadon has been gathering a vast army of evil for some ten years.'

'Fairy or Human time?' Jake said.

'Fairy time.'

'Wow, that's ...' He paused, trying to work out the maths. 'That's a long time.'

'About three thousand, six hundred and sixty human years,' Jesse said.

'Yes – that's right.' Zarlan ate an egg custard, reminding Jesse of Perigold. 'Anyway, the Union of Thirteen have been monitoring and watching the Skaardrithadon's activities. On three occasions we tried but failed to contain him. We lost *Laike du Puttchen* - a fine member of the Thirteen in one of our missions, and many Talonscarian soldiers perished also.

'The Skaardrithadon has drawn to him the most powerful dark forces from all the Fairy Kingdoms and many more evil-doers from the Unknown Kingdoms. He has released the living and dead from spells and charms we had used to keep some of the evil off the streets.'

'Dendrith and Gwendrith?' Jesse said.

'Yes, they are just two. There are many more. The Skaardrithadon has one aim: he wants to rid the kingdoms of fairies, humans, and monsters once and for all.'

'Why?' Jesse said.

'It stems from the Vampire-Fairy Wars which ended thousands of years ago. It was a terrible war, which claimed many lives. The fairy folk held power over the vampires for years, and then the shift of power changed. The vampires gained the upper-hand, stole fairy lands and enslaved the people. It was a dreadful time, but the Ancient Wizard of Elriad came from the Unknown Kingdoms and changed everything. He came with immense magic, and we were grateful to live in peace again. So, we know that one thing is certain: all fairies, humans and monsters are in terrible danger. We have no choice but to fight or run. If we run, the Skaardrithadon will take all of our homes and lands and then he will hunt us down. No one is safe. He turns all the good thoughts inside a person into madness and evil.'

Trondian-Yor nodded and retold the story about his sister's encounter with the Skaardrithadon.

'That's awful,' Jesse said again.

'What can we do to stop the Skaardrithadon?'

'There is a curse that the Ancient Wizard of Elriad used many years ago. It has since become known as the Curse of Caldazar, because it was created in Caldazar. This curse held the Skaardrithadon in a state of decay and silence for thousands of Fairy years. Indeed the Curse is still partly active, for the Skaardrithadon cannot yet leave the Sanctum where he is imprisoned beneath the twin spires. But he *is* awake and others can go to him and leave the Sanctum. Others obey his orders and do his evil deeds. His mind magic is vast.'

'Why can't he break the Curse of Caldazar totally?' Jesse asked.

'Prophesy,' Zarlan said.

'What?'

'The Ancient Wizard of Elriad who created the Curse of Caldazar also created a Double Safety Charm. This Charm was made to act like a safety net to stop the Skaardrithadon from escaping into the Fairy Kingdoms and beyond into the human world. So far it's worked, but the Prophesy says that "once all the Driths are gathered with their demons in that one place of darkness, all gathered around the Skaardrithadon, he will have enough evil power to blot out the light of the Curse." He'll unleash terror and death like no other has ever unleashed.'

'How can we stop him escaping?' Jesse said.

'There is a way, but it is incredibly dangerous.'

'Spit it out,' the Dragon Hunter said.

'The Curse of Caldazar has to be re-activated.'

'How?'

Zarlan looked around at Iggywig, the Hunter, Trondian-Yor, and his eyes finally fell on Jesse and Jake. 'The Prophesy says that in future times there will come two children of innocence: one a magical child, the other a human. Together they will chant the Curse and send the Darkness back to a safe place, and the people will rejoice and be free, but alone their Curse will be useless. Alone the Skaardrithadon will gather and harvest the people like wheat and he will rule with his magic of evil and destroy the light of many worlds.'

'Outrageous,' the Dragon Hunter said. 'They are just children. What chance do they have against such a force? I will go and dispatch this creature. I am Jesse's protector and I have killed many dragons and-'

'Please, Hunter. You are no match for the Skaardrithadon. He would gather you into his cloud of darkness and you would return either mad or as his evil servant.'

Trondian-Yor nodded.

'What if Iggywig be a-going with the brave slayer? The Curse be a-needing two to chant it, does it not?'

Zarlan shook his head.

'I wish it were so. But not even I or Trondian-Yor could replace the children. Even with our vast magic, we are no match for the Skaardrithadon. There is only one way to defeat him. And there are only two children who can re-activate the Curse of Caldazar.'

Jesse and Jake glanced at each other with eyes as wide as rabbits caught in a car's head lights.

Eleven

# The Battle for Caldazar

The huge army of the Non-Monster Alliance landed on the ridge which overlooked the sucking twin spires. They came on flying beasts led by Zarlan-Jagr and Trondian-Yor. Jesse transformed into a beautiful shiny black dragon. Jake travelled on her back.

'Trondian-Yor, Iggywig, the Dragon Hunter and a handful of our best soldiers will get you as close as they can to the Skaardrithadon,' Zarlan said. 'We will attack from both eastern and western flanks. Our efforts may prove enough of a distraction to get you into the Sanctum itself. But it will not be easy.'

'Aye, you will find a maze of passage-ways beneath the twin spires,' Androst added. 'Down there are evil beasts and monsters. Some work for the Skaardrithadon, but many have stalked the maze for years with their own concerns.'

'Be on your guard and use your wits and magic when needed,' Zarlan said. 'Remember, you need to chant the Curse together otherwise-'

'It's useless,' Jesse cut in. 'We know.' She turned to Jake. 'Are you certain you're okay about this?'

Jake nodded. He was shaking like a rattle.

'Trust in your powers and the light,' Zarlan said.

'What light?' Jesse said.

'The light inside you. It will guide you.'

'My golden glow, you mean.'

Zarlan smiled. 'Yes. It is a powerful guide. Use it.'

'How?'

'Talk to it. Tell it your troubles. It'll answer.'

'What?' Jesse couldn't hide her surprise.

''Tis true,' Iggywig said. 'Me be a-chattering to my golden glow all the time.'

'You're mad,' she said. 'Both of you. Haven't you got some practical magic we could use? Like Short-Fuse Charms, maybe?'

'An exploding charm?' Jake added.

Iggywig smiled and produced a belt which reminded Jesse of a builder's tool belt.

'Be just the thing I be a-having,' he said. ''Tis a Short-Fuse Magic Multipurpose Belt. Be a very useful.' He handed it to Jesse. She handed it to Jake.

'You need it more than I do,' she said. 'I have my shape-shifting and soothsaying.'

'You have more than that,' Zarlan said.

'The Seeing-Stone?' she said.

'Yes, use the power of the stone only as last resort. Take care, Jesse Jameson,' Zarlan said, and he hugged her as if he were going away for a very long time. 'I have passed my most precious gift on to you, fairy child. Trust its wisdom. It has guided me through the good times and the bad.'

*

Iggywig, the Dragon Hunter, Trondian-Yor and a handful of Non-Monster Alliance troops descended the cliff-face, with Jesse and Jake safely in amongst them. Zarlan and the tens of thousands of Talonscarian and fairy troops took to the skies of Caldazar. Their battle cries rang in her ears. The Vaalbosh's screaming war cries were returned and chilled her bones. The never-ending night pressed around them. The battle for Caldazar had begun.

*

Ahead, Jesse spied a bridge, guarded by a half dozen Caldazarian soldiers. She and her companions had stopped after an hour travelling around the fortified city and were now hiding in a rocky outcrop just a hundred yards away.

'This is the Northern Gateway,' Trondian-Yor explained. 'Getting you into this quarter of Caldazar isn't going to be easy. But we have friends with us. Here come Juniper and Jules. Look.'

Two enormous monsters lumbered through an archway and out onto the stone bridge. They rocked and rolled as they crossed, laughing, swearing, banging each other hard on their backs.

'Are they drunk?' Jake whispered.

'No,' said Trondian-Yor. 'They are a couple of non-monster sympathisers, who act in the amateur dramatics society here in Northern Caldazar.'

'They're actors?' Jesse couldn't stifle her surprise.

'Bad ones, but yes – that's right.'

Jesse watched in amazement as the drunken monsters argued with one another. A half dozen Caldazarian soldiers moved onto the bridge – weapons raised.

'Halt!' one soldier ordered. 'Back inside. No one is allowed out.'

The drunken monsters ignored the soldier and stumbled into the middle of the bridge.

'What did yer say?' Juniper said, pushing Jules so hard he almost toppled over the bridge's railings into the water below.

'You heard – you fat freak,' said Jules.

'Your mother was a huge lump of monster lard. She was so ugly that the sight of her could kill a Savacat at a hundred paces.'

'Why you slimy drool-gobbling muck spreading dung beetle,' Juniper yelled.

Juniper punched Jules in the stomach. He keeled over, but as he rose, Jules let loose a ferocious left hook. It hit Juniper square on his enormous crocodile jaw. SNAP.

'Break it up!' a soldier shouted.

Juniper turned on the soldier and hit him clean between his four eyes. Within seconds more non-monster sympathisers joined in the fight. Fists flew, blood flowed, pushing and shoving.

'Come on,' Trondian-Yor said, transforming into his monster self. 'Run.'

Jesse transformed into her monster self as she ran, picking up Jake, the Dragon Hunter and Iggywig under her arms. They weighed less than tiny babies.

She scurried down the outcrop, sliding through dense vegetation and dodging boulders and rocks. She followed Trondian-Yor onto the bridge. Ducking in between a Caldazarian soldier and Juniper, who were knocking lumps out of each other, she weaved her way past. Within seconds she was through the archway. She hurtled into a dark alley.

She glanced behind just as she turned into another alley. She saw Jules tossing two soldiers into the river. Juniper was howling like a mad dog, clamped on the back of a confused soldier, who was desperately trying to shake him off. 'Ride that piggy!' Juniper yelled. 'Giddy up!'

Ten minutes later, Jesse's pace slowed. She put down her companions and transformed back to her fairy self. It felt good.

They had arrived at the outer courtyard which protected the twin spires.

'Now our problems grow manifold,' Trondian-Yor said. He'd transformed into his quargkin self. 'Beyond this courtyard, there are three more inner courtyards. Each one is protected by foul beasts and creatures. The Skaardrithadon is personally protected by a Traagadon – a gigantic creature that is part wolf, part scorpion. No Caldazarian soldier or monster has ever entered these Sanctums and returned to tell the tale as flesh and blood.'

'What do they return as?' Jake wanted to know.

'Perhaps it's not wise to fill the children's heads with too much that may frighten them,' the Dragon Hunter said.

'Maybe, but they need to understand what they are up against. They will be on their guard even more.'

'I disagree.'

'I want to know,' Jesse said.

'So do I,' Jake said, his voice quivering.

'You just say that to sound brave,' the Dragon Hunter said. 'You both should be concentrating on learning the Curse.'

'I know the Curse of Caldazar off by heart,' Jesse said.

'So do I,' Jake said, nodding.

'We want to know what the Caldazarians become when they return.' Jake blinked nervously.

As Trondian-Yor opened his mouth to speak, a flurry of activity grabbed their attention. Kildrith and Jagdrith glided into view, pausing at the portcullis. The crow on the young witch's shoulder cawed anxiously and scanned the dark with its beady carrion eyes.

The iron grid gate lifted with a slow rumbling sound. Dark shadowy figures emerged at the threshold. All Jesse could see for certain were blinking blood red eyes and flashing yellow teeth.

Kildrith twisted around and stared towards

Jesse. She backed into a doorway out of sight.

'What is it?' Jagdrith said, peering in Jesse's direction.

'I smell fairies,' Kildrith said.

Jagdrith sniffed the air excitedly. 'Yes. I smell them. And a human, too.'

'A child – male.'

'Yes, do you think –'

Trondian-Yor had transformed into his monster self and ambled out of his hiding place. He stomped towards the Driths, whistling.

'Haven't seen your kind in Caldazar for a very long time,' he said casually. 'Lost are we?'

'Mind your own business, freak,' Jagdrith spat. Her crow's eyes narrowed on his throat. 'Why are you skulking about in the shadows?'

'I was going to ask you the same thing,' he said.

Kildrith's eyes glowed. 'Seen any humans or fairies back there?'

Trondian-Yor laughed. 'Why? Are you looking for some?'

The shadowy figures mumbled and muttered darkly. The portcullis began to close.

Jagdrith tossed her hair like a horse tossing its mane, wrapped her cloak around her, and disappeared into the blackness of the Sanctum.

'Be careful, freak,' Kildrith said. 'Now get out of my face before our friendly little chit-chat turns into something mean and nasty.'

Trondian-Yor turned away from the warlock. Bellowing laughter echoed along the empty alleyways. He released a dozen invisible bats from his fingers and they flew undetected into the outer courtyard.

Before the warlock could issue another word or cast a spell, Trondian-Yor vanished into the shadows. The portcullis slammed shut and Kildrith's curses faded with his footfalls.

A strange dark silence would have fallen, but for the cries of the battle in the skies above.

\*

'How do we get in?' the Dragon Hunter said. They were just a few yards from the portcullis. The only light came from an open window and a couple of houses in the near by alley.

'We could fly over the Sanctum walls,' Jesse said.

'Not advisable. Watch.' Trondian-Yor opened his palm and a small rock appeared. He threw it over the wall. There was a loud cracking sound, a flash of light, and the rock rebounded onto the cobblestone alley. It crumbled to dust.

'Tis a force field of considerable powerings,' Iggywig said. 'Be there another way a-getting the children in?'

'Bats.' Trondian-Yor said. 'Here come two now.'

Two bats flew through a tiny square opening in the portcullis. They became visible as they landed on Trondian-Yor's hand. They both chatted in a high pitched click.

'Thank you, my friends,' Trondian-Yor said, waving his hand over them. They vanished.

Trondian-Yor walked to a panel on the wall and

tapped some of the strange symbols. It was like an ATM outside her mum's bank, Jesse thought. Only instead of money coming out of the dispenser, the gate slowly rose. They entered the Outer Sanctum as quietly as they could. A few seconds later the gate slammed shut. Through the gloom Jesse could see silhouettes of statues and large ornaments which were dotted around the outer walls. Torches burned a low green light. Four archways, one on each side of the Sanctum, were like gaping mouths. In between the archway, deep alcoves hid shadowy tombs and ancient relics.

'Which way?' Jesse whispered.

'Ahead.' Trondian-Yor led the way, producing a wand from nowhere, which glowed orange at its tip.

'How do those wizards do that?' Jake said.

'Magic,' Jesse said. 'Now shut up and stay close. Can you really remember all the Curse of Caldazar?'

'Almost.'

'Almost?' Jesse couldn't disguise her disgust. 'You lied back there. You told everyone you knew it all.'

'Well … I do … kind of.'

'That's not good enough, Jake. Which bit don't you know?'

'I get mixed up on the last line … you know, the *back whence ye came* stuff.'

'Perfect,' she said. 'Back whence ye came.'

'Yeah, I know now, but the more I think about it, the more muddled I get. Whence ye back came; back ye came whence; whence back ye came? See. Which one is it?'

'BACK WHENCE YE CAME.'

'Right. Got it. I think.'

'You better have got it.' Jesse scowled. 'A lot of people are counting on us to get it right.'

'Yeah, I know,' Jake said. 'That's hard to take.'

'But we can do it. Right?'

'Sure,' Jake said, but he didn't sound convincing.

*

Zarlan-Jagr and the thousands of troops battled in the skies over Caldazar. They swooped and dived, clawed and gouged, scratched and shredded each other with hatred and malice. Zarlan weaved in and out of the Vaalbosh, issuing magic from his fingers that stunned and paralysed the hideous winged-creatures. Their death cries rang in his ears. Their final screams chilled his bones. And still he flew on through the swarms of creatures, hunting down the magic dark trail that weaved a corkscrew pattern in the bloody sky. He sought just one enemy: the leader of the chaos – Zundrith.

With uncanny accuracy he rode the corkscrew trail through the sky, with rainbow-coloured sparks flying from his boots, until he was far from the battle cries of the Vaalbosh and his own troops.

He could have been travelling days or seconds, he had no way of knowing which. His mind swirled as he twisted and twirled, holding onto the corkscrew of darkness. On and on he flew, never releasing his grip. His mind blanked as he shifted from one time and place to another. Then again he slipped into another dimension, like a set of Russian dolls where one smaller doll was lifted to reveal another even smaller one. This was the magic of time and space, he thought, but he did not let go. This is the magic the Ancient Wizard of Elriad had spoken about often in the Saga of Egornion. Such heroic adventures loomed as if real in his time-space warped mind. The Evenstorm Earthwitch's devastating rise, the cold long months of endurance in the snowy wastes of North Elriad, Oddusios the Brave and his fight against the Twisted Root of Jaarfindor. All of the heroic myths and legends came alarmingly to life.

At last he reached the mountain of icy teeth and jagged frozen water. And there, fixed to the river bank, enfolded in a dark swarming evil, the wizard came face to face with the High Witch, Zundrith.

*

The companions hurried along a narrow stone path. Just as Jesse thought they'd made it through to the next courtyard, she was hit with force across the chest. She flew backwards and fell hard. Jake was knocked sideways by another invisible force. The Dragon Hunter drew his sword of light, but he was too slow. Another unseen force knocked it from his hand and he fell like a tree. He sank to his knees. Two of the Non-Monster Alliance soldiers vanished, dragged into the shadows. Iggywig and Trondian-Yor conjured lightning rods and smashed them to the ground. The entire Outer Sanctum lit up as if floodlights had been turned on. There were screams from the unseen attackers as they retreated into the dark recesses, or slipped down drain holes.

'The Narvosh are devils in the dark,' Trondian-Yor said. 'But they will not return while the light is so strong.'

Iggywig helped Jesse to her feet. She was wheezing. Jake held his left arm.

'You all right?' Jesse asked.

'No,' Jake said. 'My arm hurts.'

'What hit us?' Jesse said.

'The full force of the Narvosh energy attack,'

Trondian said. 'We were lucky. There were only three of them. A couple of blows usually paralyse their enemies. Three attacks will maim or kill.'

'I wish I had kept my big mouth shut,' the Dragon Hunter said, staggering to his feet. 'Then I would have known more about my enemies that guard this place. I would have been prepared for their attack.'

Jesse gazed around now that light illuminated the sanctuary. The alcoves were dome-shaped, with mosaics of gruesome beasts looming down. In the centre, an unopened stone tomb dominated each alcove. Cobwebs stretched and hung everywhere. The relics were mainly bones and teeth and dried skins piled on top of the tombs. Each tomb had been carved with wild fearsome faces, bulging eyes, gaunt cheeks, and sinister open mouths.

Jesse shuddered and unlocked her gaze.

This place made her feel extremely uncomfortable, but the pain in her chest was worse. She coughed and held her hand over the pain. She wished it would go away. Oh, how she wished it would go away.

'Jesse!' Jake shouted. 'Look! Your hand is on fire!'

Jesse looked down at her hand. It glowed yellow-orange-red. Where she had it clamped over her chest, she could feel a growing heat. Her palm tingled. Her hand glowed brighter. She felt calm, not panicked like Jake.

'Look, Trondian! Jesse's on fire!'

Trondian-Yor placed a comforting hand on

Jake's shoulder. 'It's okay, Jake.'

'No, it's not! She'll burn to death! Do something! Someone do something!'

'What's going on, wizard?' the Dragon Hunter said, an edge to his voice.

'It's one of Jesse's magic powers, one of her new powers emerging from the Seeing-Stone when it's needed.'

'Tis a wondrous sighting,' Iggywig said. 'Jesse be a-healing herself.'

It was true, Jesse thought. It was incredible. She was healing the pain in her chest. It was like a circle of hurt the size of a dinner plate, which now shrivelled smaller and smaller to the size of a penny.

Then gone.

The lights in her hand vanished.

Instinctively, she reached out and found Jake's wound. Her hand tingled as if a small current of electricity ran through it. It glowed again and within seconds his throbbing had vanished, too.

'Very impressive, golden glow girl,' Jagdrith hissed from the darkness of the next Inner Sanctum. 'But you'll need more healing hands than an octopus by the time we've finished with you!'

*

Zundrith didn't seem to notice Zarlan-Jagr at first. She was fixed intently on her visions. She had two. One was locked on the glorious battle in the never-ending night of the Caldazarian sky, and the other was urging on the Driths who were about to unleash their dark magic on the child, Jesse, and the buffoons the fairy child called friends.

'Step an inch closer, wizard,' she hissed without turning, 'and I will kill you where you stand.'

'You know why I am here, witch,' Zarlan-Jagr said. 'Call off your army and release Perigold and the rest of the Union of Thirteen you've cursed to sleep.'

Zundrith howled with mock laughter. 'What a fool you are, wizard. You have ridden the Dark Trail of Time to be here with me because of a misplaced hunch.'

'You lie.'

'No, you lie to yourself. My power has nothing to do with your precious Union of Thirteen. As for Perigold, I hope he rots in that chamber beneath Talonscar.'

'How do you know about Talonscar if it were not you who cursed him?'

'I know many things, but your Union is too small to concern me. And as for my army, I shall not call them off until they have destroyed every last one of your trooping fairies and Talonscarian scum. The pleasure I feel from witnessing the deaths of thousands is such a satisfying one. Life to give, life to take. You know what I mean, wizard. You too have killed and maimed with your magic in the name of your precious Union, have you not?'

Zarlan ignored her.

'Who holds Perigold, if it is not you?' he said.

'Do I look like I care?'

Zarlan moved closer.

'Step another inch nearer to me and I shall kill you where you stand, wizard.'

Zarlan-Jagr laughed. 'You plan to kill me anyway, witch. Why play games?'

'It amuses me.'

'Yes, I suppose it does. Stuck here, as you have been for so long, must make you desire for all kinds of amusement.'

'A smart mouth like yours needs to learn respect,' she growled, and turned impossibly as if her head were an owl. 'A smart mouth like yours, little wizard, will pay for your smart quips.'

Zarlan felt it coming before he saw it. The High Witch released the full force of her glaring hate-riddled eyes. Tornadoes of black energy twisted through the air quicker than he had anticipated. They hit his chest, knocking him a hundred feet into the air. He cartwheeled over and over, slamming hard against the far bank. Sparks flew from his boots and he felt the bitter-sweet metallic taste of blood in his mouth. His head was spinning wildly. Her power had shocked him. One more blow from her and he knew that he would be finished.

*

The blonde witch's face lit up like a bonfire. Her crow cawed darkly and flapped its wings. Kildrith and Gwendrith appeared either side of her. Their eyes were red with rage and they snarled. Wasps spewed from Gwendrith's ghostly mouth.

'Kill them all!' Kildrith screamed.

Trondian-Yor threw a handful of lightning rods into the Inner Sanctum, and then rushed in. Jesse,

Jake and Iggywig hurried close behind. The Nardvosh scurried into any dark crevice they could find. The Dragon Hunter unleashed his sword of light as he strode in next. He was surrounded by grotesque creatures, which were not afraid of the light.

'Helgvosh!' Iggywig yelled. 'Be only one way to killing them!'

'And what's that?' the Dragon Hunter said, spinning his sword in an arc. He sliced off the heads of three Helgvosh. They exploded into green vapour and disappeared.

'Tis the way, kind slayer.' Iggywig applauded. 'Be a-taking off Helgvosh's heads.'

'There's the human you smelled,' Jagdrith said, pointing at Jake. She raised her hands into claws and waved them at him. Her crow cawed menacingly. 'Vile, stinking human child. Come to me, so I can crush your bones to dust and ashes.'

Jake yelled and tried to back away behind Jesse, but he slid forward, lassoed by an invisible force. Jagdrith's hate-filled mucus-covered eyes loomed larger and larger. Jake turned and started to run but it was hopeless. It was as if he were running on an escalator backwards. The young witch held out her hands. Her crow jumped up and down, digging its sharp claws into her shoulder. Jake slid faster and faster now towards her.

Kildrith fired a bolt of lightning from his fingertips. Jesse dived to her right as the lightning whizzed-crackled inches above her head. It hit a tomb with a crunching sound and a huge hole appeared. Pieces of stone and dust exploded inside the alcove. A great whooshing noise was followed by a thick crimson mist spewing out of the tomb. From the mist towered three fearsome creatures, ghosts of the ancient dead, soulless demons possessed by the evil force of the Skaardrithadon.

'Blaaarrghast!' they cried.

Kildrith shot scores of lightning bolts at the tombs. More ancient dead rose from dark holes and within moments they surrounded Jesse and her companions.

Jagdrith grabbed Jake around his waist tightly and lifted him up.

'Squeeze the life out of the brat,' Kildrith said.

'Yes, but not too quickly,' Gwendrith cackled. 'Make him suffer, as I shall make that gobbit suffer!'

Gwendrith shot like a cannonball up into the air and rebounded off the vaulted ceiling. She landed in front of Iggywig, eyes blazing, claws outstretched above her head.

The ancient dead closed in, too.

Kildrith and Jagdrith howled with demonic laughter. Jake's breath was slipping from his lungs. He was being crushed to death.

Trondian-Yor wriggled his fingers and a burst of fire encircled them. The intensity of the flames became hotter and brighter. The ancient dead squealed and retreated into their tombs. Gwendrith didn't seem to notice the flames, as she pounced on Iggywig. But Iggywig leapt high into the air, as if his legs were springs. He stuck to the ceiling like a fly, arms and legs splayed. Gwendrith tried to fly up, but the circle of fire had somehow stopped her. She turned on Trondian-Yor, snarling, but the young quargkin wizard pushed out his hand. A glass egg tumbled to the floor and stopped at Gwendrith's feet. She looked at him with a mixture of malice and disbelief. Then she looked at the egg and screamed.

'No!'

But it was too late. Her ghostly energy was sucked into the egg in a millisecond. She was imprisoned again.

Trondian-Yor bent down and picked up the egg. He tossed it to Jesse.

'Take her with you. Do with her as you please. Now go! Get through the next two Inner Sanctums and you'll be in the company of the Skaardrithadon. You know what to do.'

Jesse nodded. 'What about Jake?'

Trondian-Yor glanced up at the ceiling. Jesse followed his gaze. Iggywig had gone.

Across the Sanctum, they now saw that Iggywig had snatched Jake back. He must have surprised them, dropping from the ceiling onto the unsuspecting Driths.

'Return the child!' Jagdrith yelled.

Iggywig ignored her demand and unleashed three Short-Fuse Charms from Jake's tool belt. First, a thick fog rose up and enveloped the warlock and witch. They coughed and spluttered inside the blue smoke, swearing and cursing. A small ball rolled into the fog, exploded and hundreds of chains shot out. The Driths yelled.

When the fog cleared, Jesse was pleased to see them wrapped in metal from head to toe.

'Go now!' Trondian-Yor ordered. 'We'll do what we can to stop them from following you.'

Jesse grabbed Jake's hand, kissing Iggywig as she raced by into the darkness of the second Inner Sanctum. She couldn't bear to wave at the Dragon Hunter, for fear she would never see him again. She heard the buzz of his sword of light as he dispatched three attacking creatures.

'I am your guardian in this world and the next, Jesse Jameson!' he shouted after her. 'Don't ever forget that. No one will pass by me this day!'

As Jesse led Jake deeper into the darkness, hurtling through the Inner Sanctums, she answered the Dragon Hunter in her head. *I could never forget you! How could I ever forget any of my friends?*

But within the next few steps, she'd forgotten everything, except the chilling cloud of darkness which welcomed her at the doorway to the Innermost Sanctum.

It was there that the Skaardrithadon prowled like a starving beast, eager for its kill.

## Twelve

# Cloud of Darkness

Zarlan-Jagr mustered all of his strength and got slowly to his feet. His legs felt like deep sea diver's boots. He spat blood out from his sore mouth. He opened his bleary eyes expecting to see Zundrith issue her final volley of dark magic to finish him off, but he was greeted by something of equal horror.

There was a harsh screech from behind him, and unseen trapdoors flapped and banged in the shadows. Maligned creatures leapt out. Demons of fur and metal. Ghouls with claws and talons. Creatures so grotesque and vile, so malformed and ugly, that his mind could not understand their hideousness. Each one carried a weapon.

'Kill him,' Zundrith cackled. 'Then eat him.'

Zarlan-Jagr's response was automatic. He swivelled on his heels while his fingertips cast forth sparks and fire and magic.

A dozen creatures wailed as they took the full force of his wizardry. They were bowled back into the shadows from where they came.

Weapons soared through the air, and hailed on him. He slipped on the bank, staggered, shoved them off. Three spiky balls with hard handles hit his back as he tried to climb the slippery bank. He knew he had been wounded. He felt the sticky warm blood running down his spine, but he had to get to higher ground to stand a chance. His wounds would have to wait.

A demon lurched forward, its neck stretching out like rubber from its waif-like shoulders, and screamed in his face. Its hot rancid breath made him gag.

'Break every bone in his sorry wizard's body!' Zundrith bawled.

Handfuls of his cloak were ripped from him, slashed by vicious teeth. Other frozen hands clasped his ankles as he tried to scramble up the icy bank. He kicked them off, but still the demons and creatures came in their hundreds from the dark places around the High Witch. She summoned them with spells and incantations, and they came, came riding on the backs of winged devils screaming destruction.

*

Jesse Jameson led the charge.

'That was too easy,' Jake said. 'We got here without a single problem.'

'He let us,' Jesse said, nodding to the dark cloud that hovered at the end of the Sanctum. 'He wants us now. The longer this battle goes on, the weaker he becomes.'

'How do you know that?' Jake asked.

Jesse shrugged.

'Very perceptive, Jesse Jameson,' the Skaardrithadon said. His voice was surprisingly normal – no lisp, or wheeze, or hiss. 'But you are wrong.'

Jesse laughed. 'You grow stronger? I don't think so.'

'Think what you will, but watch your back.' The Skaardrithadon gave out a hideous demonic laugh. His cloud rumbled.

Jesse heard a scraping noise. She remembered Trondian's words as if a bullet had whizzed by her ear: *the Skaardrithadon is protected by a fearsome Traagadon.* Turning, she saw behind her a frightening sight. The Traagadon was enormous. It had the head of a lobster, the body, tail and pincers of a black gleaming scorpion, and the limbs of a giant wolf. Strangely it was covered in a fine black gossamer fur. Its movements were quick and jerky. Its head touched the ceiling. Rivers of foamy white spittle ran from its serrated beak.

'Bring them to me,' the Skaardrithadon commanded the Traagadon.

'Stand back,' Jesse said, pushing Jake aside. 'I'll deal with this.'

'Er … all right,' Jake said stupidly. 'Are you sure you don't need help?'

'Certain. Move away.'

Jake backed off.

The Traagadon moved closer, its gleaming black eyes staring bleakly from stalks. Jake inched further away. Jesse stood her ground. The Traagadon reared up, blowing fire and smoke like a dragon. Despite her surprise, Jesse didn't budge. She knew what she had to do.

The Traagadon began its attack.

But before Jesse could transform into a creature of greater menace and power, Jake panicked and threw down two Short-Fuse Charms from his belt.

'What are you doing, you idiot!' Jesse yelled. 'You haven't got a clue what the charms will do!'

'I know,' Jake smirked, turning. 'Sorry. Run like the clappers!'

*

Scrambling on top of the bank, Zarlan-Jagr turned to face the multitude of demons. He exploded his way through them, running as the creatures tumbled, his fingers like gun barrels, shooting magic as if bullets which knocked down the demons with simple ease.

'Stop him!' Zundrith cried.

But they could not stop him. The wizard's fingers shot lightning bolts and energy bursts, which sent the demons skulking back into the shadows. Zarlan's magic frightened them, the hundreds who had continued to pursue him. They hesitated, glanced at each other for support. They heard the High Witch's orders to attack and kill and eat!

Some broke ranks and raced towards Zarlan-Jagr. Their hunger for wizard flesh was greater than their fear of him. Once more, they attacked with a fresh purpose.

'That's right, my pathetic little retinue,' Zundrith cackled. 'Hunt him down! Bring him to his knees!'

Zarlan backed away, light on his feet, swerving his body like a rugby player to avoid the flying weapons. He shot forth flames and lightning bolts as he went. He hit many demons, but still they came from the darkness as if a dam of evil had burst. They flew up and around him, circling like vultures.

Now they attacked with greater malice, but he held his ground. There was nowhere to run, except along the river bank to the waterfall. He was already frozen to the bone, and didn't relish the thought of an ice cold drenching. No, he would stand and fight.

He uttered charms and spells, ancient and unheard for thousands of years.

They screamed and shrieked and spat and clawed at him, trying to drag him down like a lion might drag its prey. But he conjured more ancient fire and flame from his sizzling fingertips, and at last the demons tired, fell, squealed, scurried back to the dark pits from where they came.

'BRING HIM DOWN!' Zundrith shouted, but her demons had deserted her. 'Kill him! Don't skulk and hide! Kill him!'

But they didn't dare leave their pits.

All that stood between the High Witch and Zarlan-Jagr was the crazed black figure emerging from the shadows. It was the witch's brother, Dumdrith.

With terrific speed he snapped his neck. He cracked bone and sinew at the base of his skull. A mouth filled with rotten gnashing teeth snarled between a mass of tangled red hair. And that mouth was a disgusting thing, opening and shutting at the back of his head like a machine.

'Finish him, you dim-wit,' Zundrith growled.

For a second, Zarlan hesitated, shocked by the sight of Dumdrith. He had seen many weird and bizarre creatures in his long life and travels, but this one defied even his wild imagination.

His hesitation was a mistake.

Dumdrith lurched forward with the agility and speed of a panther. Before the wizard had time to react, Dumdrith had pinned him against the ice and snow. He cracked his neck, twisting it so that his snapping jaws leered at the wizard's exposed throat. He plunged forward to bite the life from Zarlan, but the wizard regained his senses just in time. He flung the creature from him sideways and skipped to his feet. As Dumdrith scrambled to his feet, Zarlan pushed out both hands and a rippling energy tore the fabric of time. Dumdrith was bowled over like a pin and when he staggered up again, he was just a child. His mouth was back in its rightful place and his childish innocence back in his eyes. He still had a shock of flame red hair, and he looked at the wizard and the High Witch with strange fascination.

'Where am I?' Dumdrith said in a small bewildered voice. He did not recognise either of them. For all he knew, he could have been dreaming. Perhaps he was.

'Walk away, through there,' Zarlan said, pointing to a blue door that had appeared just to his left. 'Go back home.'

'He is home,' Zundrith said. 'Now undo that spell and return him as he was.'

'Go home, son,' Zarlan said, ignoring the witch. 'Run through that door before it's too late! There are witches and demons here! Run, boy! RUN! RUN! RUN! Run home to your mother and father! That's it! Run!'

Like children the world over, the urge to run

gripped Dumdrith. He hurtled towards the door.

'Stop, you imbecile!' Zundrith roared. 'You are my brother! You have been charmed! Come back!'

'Don't listen to her. I have broken you free from your nightmare. Run, Dumdrith! Run! While you still have the chance! Run!'

The child crashed through the blue door into his past, another time and place, smiling with his new lips and mouth.

Zarlan wriggled and clicked his fingers and the door vanished. He swirled around on his heel and faced the High Witch.

'Just me and you,' he said evenly.

'You will pay with your life, wizard,' Zundrith said, raising her taloned hands above her head. A frozen blasting wind roared up from the folds of her cloak and smashed the wizard hard in his face. His white hair billowed like a horse's tail. 'And your death will be painful and slow!'

*

There was nowhere to run, except into the Sanctum where the New Master's cloud of darkness smouldered like a damp bonfire.

The first Short-Fuse Charm exploded with a dazzling blue-white light. Sparks mushroomed over the creature and took hold of its fine fur. Little licking flames danced in search of air, and quickly fanned into tongues of twisted flame. The Traagadon reared up on its hind legs and roared, shooting a jet of fire at the children.

Jesse dived on top of Jake, and they rolled clear of the blast. She felt the heat singe the back of her head. That was close, she thought, scrambling to her feet.

The Traagadon was shrouded in fire and smoke. But that only seemed to infuriate it more. It thrust out its neck and its head materialized from the smoke, stalk eyes dark pits of anger and rage. Another blast of fire whooshed from its beak.

This time Jesse transformed into a giant armour-plated golden dragon. She shielded Jake with her wings. The jet of fire rebounded off the plating and briefly lit up the Skaardrithadon's Innermost Sanctum. What she saw disturbed her but she couldn't think about it now. The Traagadon had squeezed into the Innermost Sanctum. It raised its snapping pincers to strike, serrated beak unhinged to rip and tear Jesse's armour plating ...

Bang! The second Short-Fuse Charm emptied like a gushing hydrant. Instead of torrents of water pouring into the Sanctum, an arcing gust of sonic wind blew the creature off its feet and smashed it hard into the wall. Its shell cracked. Thick white puss oozed from the cracks. It slumped, twitched, its pincers clicked, then stopped. The fire and its life were extinguished.

'Very good, human child,' the Skaardrithadon said from within his darkening cloud. 'You are a noddy, as well as a lucky charm weaver. Let's see how you fare now.'

As if covered in butter, Jake slipped from Jesse's grasp, carried across the Sanctum by an invisible force. His legs and arms flailed wildly. He screamed for Jesse's help, but it was too late. Jake disappeared into the cloud of darkness.

'Say the Curse!' Jesse yelled, transforming into her fairy self. 'Now!'

'He who caused pain, suffering and disease,' they chanted together. 'He who robbed millions to feed his greed; he who made misery, despair and killed hope; go now ... back ...'

Jake's voice faded away.

'No!' shouted Jesse. 'Don't forget it now!'

But Jake hadn't forgotten the Curse. Something else was happening. Jake shot out of the cloud and rolled like a ball to stop at Jesse's feet.

'Jake!' Jesse helped him up. He stumbled, clung to her, breathless. 'What happened?'

'It's ... it's ...' he stammered.

The words just wouldn't come.

Jesse looked at the cloud, to where Jake was nodding frantically.

'It's him ...' Jake managed, and slipped from Jesse's grip.

Jesse's jaw dropped.

The cloud moved rapidly to the far side of the Sanctum, exposing a pool of black slime. The Bogie Beast rose slowly out of the goo.

*

'Kleegnath!' Zundrith cursed in the tongue of High Witches. 'Roaarghaarm! Kilyamahtarg!'

Zarlan-Jagr threw his hands up instinctively and leapt twenty feet into the air. He somersaulted with the speed and precision of an Olympic gymnast. The three dark Death Discs which flew like Frisbees from Zundrith's eyes narrowly missed his head. But he wasn't so lucky with the next volley. He parried two Death Discs but the third ripped deep into his chest and upper arm. He hit the hard snow with a dull thump. Blood oozed out and the snow drank it greedily.

'Slow and painful,' Zundrith said again. 'Not so clever now, are we, wizard?'

Zarlan's face was numbed by the snow. He tried to turn himself over, but his right arm was useless.

'Get up and look at me!' Zundrith demanded.

Zarlan only wished he could get up, but his limbs wouldn't obey his mind. He lay twitching and frozen in the reddening snow.

'Up! Face me! I want your eyes to see me laughing as you leave this world.'

She has me, he thought. She can kill me any time she wishes. It's over. He felt a dream like horror wash over him.

'Get up!'

He tried to move his leg, to roll himself onto his back. At least he would die with some dignity, he thought. Not his face stuffed in blood and snow.

'Up!'

He managed to shift his weight to his right leg and dug his heel into the snow. He pushed as hard as he could and flipped himself over at the same time. He screamed out in agony, a burning, searing pain shooting across his chest.

'Painful and slow,' Zundrith cackled. Green drool of excitement dripped from her puckered lips.

'You sent my Sister in Suffering, Dendrith, to her death, and imprisoned her in that hellish glass egg. You will pay for her pain.' She paused and glared into the waterfall, where visions and portents could be seen. The Battle of Caldazar raged harder than ever. 'So tell me, where's your magic now, wizard? Where's your precious Union of Thirteen when you need them, eh?'

He coughed and spluttered, tasting the metallic bitter-sweetness of blood. He began to smile. The dream-like horror intensified. He felt his life force slip, seep from him a little.

'What's so funny?' she said, annoyed.

'You,' he managed. 'You have no idea what my death means, have you?'

'Riddles and puzzles, wizard. You speak them to play for time. But I am no fool. I shall end this right now!'

Zundrith's eyes glowed like red rubies and three more Death Discs cannoned out of them.

Zarlan braced himself for death, grinning.

But instead of death, came another life. The snow and blood and pain melted away. His golden glow soared up, up, up high into the cloudless grey sky. Beneath him he saw his old motionless body and Zundrith cackling gleefully. She had no idea that she'd freed him. To her, he was dead and gone, another enemy defeated. But Zarlan-Jagr had become much more than flesh and blood and wizard – he was now pure energy, with a will and purpose mere mortals would call supernatural. He had the mighty power of earthquake and hurricane, lightning and thunder, and much more beside.

Zarlan-Jagr broke through Zundrith's dimension as if ripping threadbare linen with his hands and re-entered the battling skies of Caldazar. To the Talonscarians, Vaalbosh, Zundrith's demons, and fairies that saw him, he appeared as if an angel, or some wild holy vision. His golden glow burned as bright as a star and his voice boomed like an explosion.

'The war is over!' he roared. 'Put down your weapons and return to your homes. The killing is done.'

To them all, he appeared to be speaking in their own tongue. To their eyes he looked like their own god or goddess, and they felt blessed and at peace, and many fell to their knees and prayed or wept. But to Zarlan-Jagr – now an ascended member of the Union of Thirteen – he had taken one small step of many on a never-ending White Road. He was closer than most to the truth of himself, but further from the trivialities of mortals. And with his new form, he walked through walls and flew faster than light, but he was never far from the White Wizards who had sworn to fight evil and the Dark Ones until the Great Balancing had at last been restored.

\*

'You?' Jesse couldn't hide her confusion. She glanced down at Jake. His eyelids fluttered open.

'He was still inside me,' Jake said. 'All this time, he was hiding inside me.'

'What?' Jesse said, stunned.

'A piece of me was still inside the child,' the Bogie Beast said, grinning.

Jesse glared at him with dark contempt.

'Those witches destroyed the rest of me back in the smuggler's caves on the Island Gloom.'

Jesse briefly recalled the memory. She and Jake had escaped the caves, while Dendrith, Gwendrith and the Bogie Beast had battled in the dark. Zarlan had dealt with Dendrith as she had emerged from the caves.

'And I shall destroy the rest of you,' the Skaardrithadon said. 'Or maybe you wish to join me? Your aura is certainly dark and evil enough.'

Jesse said the magic word in her mind which Zarlan had given her. The Bogie Beast's aura came into view. It was almost lightless, a dark muddy grey, streaked with black and red as if paint had been splattered into it. Its dark evil disturbed her and she quickly uttered the magic word in her head to turn off her Magiceye.

'Did you come here to join with me?' the Skaardrithadon said.

The Bogie Beast grimaced. 'And my daughter? What would become of her if I joined you?'

'I am not your daughter,' Jesse said.

'Oh, but you are, my child. The facts can never be denied. I will always be a part of you – one half fairy and one half Bogie Beast.'

'No!'

'Yes, and now I'll prove my love for you.'

'You have no love inside of you,' Jesse said acidly.

'Oh, but that is where you are wrong.' The Bogie Beast rose higher and higher, like a black stalagmite. 'Watch what I will do in the name of love.'

The Skaardrithadon knew a split second before the Bogie Beast's attack what was coming. Forks of lightning zigzagged out from the cloud.

They struck the Bogie Beast in three separate places. He screamed in agony, shrank to a quarter of his size. But he did not retreat into his pool of slime. Instead he leapt head first into the cloud, screaming. The cloud lit up and went dark. Tiny glimmers of jagged purple-white lightning twisted, deep rumbling thunder shook the floor.

Jesse dragged Jake further away to the edge of the Sanctum. She stayed clear of the horrors she'd seen slithering up and down the walls earlier.

Another crack of thunder was followed by a shower of slime. It splattered Jesse's face. She wiped it away with her hands, gagging at the stench. It was beyond comparison, stinking more than any sewer or rotten fish or vegetables.

'Wake up, Jake,' she said, shaking his shoulders. 'Come on.'

Jake did not move.

'Jake!'

Still Jake remained unconscious.

'We have to say the Curse together.' She slapped his face hard. 'Wake up!'

Jake stirred, held a hand to his stinging cheek.

'Did you hear me?'

'What?' Jake said stupidly.

'The Curse? Remember? We have to-'

'I know what we have to do,' he said, and they turned and faced the cloud.

'Let's do it,' Jesse said.

The cloud exploded with more thunderous rumbles and screams. Lightning spiked across the Sanctum floor like the tongue of an electric snake.

'Now!'

'I've forgotten the last line,' Jake said. 'Which way round is it?'

'Back whence ye came.'

'That's it. Back ... whence ye ... came.'

They chanted together.

'He who caused pain, suffering and disease; he who robbed millions to feed his greed; he who made misery, despair, and killed hope; go now back whence ye-'

The Dragon Hunter and Iggywig burst into the Sanctum, trading blows and magic with Kildrith and Jagdrith and a dozen vile mutant magic demons they had created.

Jesse pushed Jake to the floor.

Jagdrith side-stepped a thrust from the Dragon Hunter's sword and released a stream of lethal purple light from her hand. It missed the Dragon Hunter by a couple of inches and struck the wall behind him. The wall imploded and chunks of stone and rubble cascaded down. A lump of stone cracked the back of Jake's head as he nodded at Jesse to begin the Curse again. He collapsed in a heap, blood oozing from his wound.

Jesse scrambled over to his side. She shouted

his name as loud as she could, trying to rise above the racket of the battle and magic. Jake did not move. He was breathing – just – but he was unconscious.

A deafening roar came from within the cloud. An explosion of light forced Jesse to cover her eyes. When she opened them, she saw the Skaardrithadon, striding with a cock-sure arrogance out of the cloud. My God, Jesse thought, hypnotised by his slicked-back dark raven hair. His stark white face made his large black eyes seem even larger. He stood fully eight feet tall. His lips were narrow and blood-red. He wore a long swishing black cloak and black knee length leather boots. My God, she thought, unable to wrench her eyes from his long bloody fangs, he's a vampire! A giant vampire!

The Skaardrithadon threw down the dead body of the Bogie Beast at Jesse's feet.

'There's no choice,' he said without feeling. He licked his lips and blood oozed from his mouth, trickling down his chin. 'It's over for you and your friends.'

Jesse glanced across towards the victorious Driths – Jagdrith and Kildrith. They were slowly encircling Iggywig and the Dragon Hunter, who were cowering down on their haunches, hands protecting their heads. They were charmed and defeated.

'Hand it over,' Jagdrith said, gliding beside Jesse, and she opened her taloned hand. 'Give me the glass egg. Now!'

Jesse delved into her bulging pocket, dug it out and gave it to the blonde witch. She also felt her obsidian Seeing-Stone, and remembered Trondian's words about it: *when you need it most, when your back is against the wall, and there seems to be no way out – then you will know what I mean.*

Jagdrith threw the egg hard against the wall and the glass shattered. Gwendrith flew up in a howl of delight and materialized beside Jagdrith. She fixed her ghostly eyes on Iggywig.

Kildrith bent down and picked up the Dragon Hunter's sword of light as if taking sweets from a baby. The sword buzzed like a chainsaw. He raised it above his head, locking his eyes on the Dragon Hunter.

'No!' Jesse screamed. 'Leave my friends alone.'

'Not possible, child,' he said smugly. 'But take a look in that tomb over there by the door. A gift to Jesse Jameson from the Skaardrithadon, to show that I have a soft spot for the fairy folk after all.'

Jesse hurried across to the open tomb, but hesitated.

'What's wrong, child? Scared that death might look you in the eye?'

Jesse's heart pounded faster as she gingerly stepped forward and peered over the rim of the tomb. It was Perigold! He was alive! He was ... smiling ... and slowly rising up with his arms outstretched to greet her. 'Perigold!' she shouted gleefully. 'You're awake! But how did you get here?'

Perigold's smile curled into a grimace. He hissed and spat, revealing long bloody fangs. His eyes were vacant and cold and amber. Vampire!

He climbed out of the tomb, stood next to Jesse.

'No!' Jesse yelled, falling back, her chest constricting. She looked at Perigold with extreme anguish and horror plastered on her face. She turned to glare at the grinning Skaardrithadon. 'What have you done to him?'

'Your soothsaying grandfather has decided to join us,' the Skaardrithadon laughed. 'He has acquired quite a taste for blood over the past few days.'

Jesse's throat was as dry as desert sand. She eased the Seeing-Stone out of her pocket. 'He would never join you!'

The Skaardrithadon nodded. 'True. Not of his own free will. But one bite changed all that.'

Jesse's head was spinning. She glanced around to Iggywig and the Dragon Hunter for support but they were still cowering like sheep. She gripped the Seeing-Stone tightly. Why wouldn't it work? Where was her mighty magic when she needed it most?

'Should I kill them, Master?' Kildrith said, without moving his gaze from his prisoners. 'Or would you prefer to entertain them inside your cloud?'

'Hmmm,' the Skaardrithadon pretended to consider the matter. 'Difficult choice. But today I think you should kill them.'

'No!' Jesse screamed. She turned to run towards her friends, but Perigold's ice-cold hand snared her wrist like a handcuff.

'Kill them all,' the Skaardrithadon said calmly, and he twisted around, cloak swirling, and strode towards his cloud without looking back.

Trondian-Yor stepped out from the shadows, closely followed by the tracker, Kumo Diaz.

'There will be no more killing today,' Trondian-Yor said. In his hand he held a small black pyramid. 'Remember this?'

The Skaardrithadon froze.

Jesse broke free of Perigold's grip.

'No!' the Skaardrithadon hissed. His eyes widened with terror. 'That is not the Obsidian Container.'

Trondian-Yor nodded, smiling.

'You lie! It's not possible. I destroyed that hell-hole so that I would never be imprisoned in there again.'

'Yes, you did destroy one Obsidian Container,' Trondian-Yor agreed. 'But this is a twin Container – a secret reserve that only the Union of Thirteen knew about. The Ancient Wizard of Elriad who created them was a wise wizard. He out-smarted you.'

'No! NO!'

The Skaardrithadon lunged out, grabbed Perigold, and hauled him across the Sanctum. They flew into the cloud like bats retreating into the blackness of their roost.

'You know what you have to do, Jesse Jameson,' Trondian-Yor said.

'Yes, but ... Perigold?' She couldn't hide her confusion.

'Shake him from your mind. There is a chance that Perigold can be saved. But we do not have long. The effects of the vampire blood infecting him, coursing through his veins, will transform him forever. Then he will be lost.'

'How long do we have?'

'Two – maybe three days. It depends how he fights the vampire blood cells.'

'Then we must hurry,' Jesse said, regaining her composure somewhat. She absently rubbed her cold wrist and upper arm where a piece of shadow had been ripped from her by a Shadow Eater.

Trondian-Yor tossed the Obsidian Container toward her. She caught it in one hand and raised the other, aiming the glowing Seeing-Stone as if a gun. Like a fairy with a fire-arm, her flesh began to glow red, then yellow and orange. The Seeing-Stone imploded, embedded itself into her hand, fusing flesh and obsidian together. From her palm erupted an ocean of sparks and storm. The Driths were bowled over like skittles. Her magical powers had multiplied manifold, amplified by the Obsidian Container and the Seeing-Stone. The charm around the Dragon Hunter and Iggywig was broken.

It took a few moments for them to shake the spell completely from their minds.

'You are right, my friend,' Jesse said to Iggywig. She had never felt more confident, never felt as strong as she did now. 'A long time ago you said that the Fairy Kingdoms were jam packed with magic.'

'Tis true, as you be a-finding out.'

'Ready?' she said.

All of her companions nodded.

Jesse Jameson leapt into the darkness of the vampire's cloud, repeating over and over the Curse of Caldazar. Carrying a limp Jake in his arms, the Dragon Hunter followed Iggywig, Kumo Diaz, and Trondian-Yor into the cloud. The greatest battle the Fairy Kingdoms had ever seen was about to begin.

# Jesse Jameson

## and the Curse of Caldazar

### Glossary

**Accounted** - able to be explained; in this case a record of the Union of Thirteen.

**Ascended** - to have climbed or risen, to have moved upward.

**ATM** - automatic transaction machines dispense cash at banks – sometimes called *holes in the wall.*

**Aura** - invisible breath, emanation, or radiation that seems to surround a person or thing.

**Code of Conduct** - to live by a set of rules and ways to act and think.

**Descended** - to have gone down, to lower oneself.

**Dons** - once had great power in the Naargapire. They ruled like lords and kept the ordinary folk in slavery. (See Skaardrithadon).

**Driths** - dark witches and warlocks, a race of spiteful magical folk.

**Guardian spirit** - in many myths, legends and folktales these entities protect woods, or mountains, or any part of the landscape. It is traditional to offer a gift to gain their favour.

**Mage** - a magician or sorcerer.

**Magiceye** - the ability to see other creatures' auras and know things about them.

**Obsidian** - a usually black or banded, hard volcanic glass that displays shiny, curved surfaces when fractured and is formed by rapid cooling of lava. Traditionally used as a Seeing-Stone in many ancient cultures.

**Portal** - door or gateway into another dimension or parallel world.

**Prophesy** - to predict a future event.

**Retinue** - followers.

**Seeing-Stone** - traditionally used for magical acts, such as looking into the future or other dimensions, or to store magic and power.

**Skaardrithadon** - a mysterious creature that has a taste for blood and a lust for power.

**Skogsra** - a woodland fairy, a beautiful creature with a foxtail. Sometimes helpful, sometimes harmful. From Scandinavian folklore.

**Transcended** - to go beyond; to excel; to surpass.

Excerpt from Book 4

*Jesse Jameson and the Vampire Vault*

## One

# The Wild Hunt

The Skaardrithadon glided deeper and deeper into stifling cloud, and Jesse flew after him. All she could think about was Perigold, now a vampire slave. The thought made her feel sick. In her hands, Jesse Jameson held the black obsidian pyramid. Each time she closed the gap between them, its point flashed blood red. Once it had lit up a luminous green and stopped flashing. She had been within a few hundred yards of him, but somehow in the foggy mirk he'd escaped again. Still she flew on as her dragon self.

Jesse glanced over her spiny shoulder and looked at her companions. It had been a long and difficult journey in the gloomy mists of the Skaardrithadon's ever expanding aura. But they had not faltered. Trondian-Yor and Iggywig were flying together besides a winged beast the wizard had fashioned from the ether of his magical mind. It was big and powerful, black and scaly, a cross between an eagle, a dragon, a horse and a tortoise. Its shell was speckled and enormous. Giant eagle wings flapped slowly and its six horse legs galloped for added speed.

Iggywig called the power of the creature's legs his 'turbo boostings.' Its noble head was that of a dragon, able to breathe fire and brimstone. Trondian-Yor had named his creature creation Cyren, because it wailed like a fire engine at approaching danger.

Behind them, sitting astride Cyren's tortoise shell back, the Dragon Hunter cradled Jake in his arms. Jake had not regained consciousness since he'd blacked out in the Innermost Sanctum back at Caldazar. Kumo Diaz sat astride the creature's neck, holding reins and looking as if he was steering, but both he and the others knew who was boss: Cyren had a mind of his own.

Jesse had no idea where they were now. They could have travelled for hours or days. There was no way of telling except Jesse was starving hungry and thirsty. Her mouth was as dry as an oven and it was painful to lick her lips because her tongue was tender and had swollen up.

'We should rest awhile,' Trondian-Yor said, breaking the silence.

'No,' Jesse said, gaze locked on the luminous wafer-thin trail. 'We are getting closer.'

'True,' Kumo Diaz said. 'But Trondian speaks sense. We stop now for a while.'

Jesse ignored them, increasing her pace, wings flapping like great rhythmic heart beats. At the front of her thoughts was her grandfather, Perigold. She had to release him from his vampire state. Time was running out. Perhaps, it had already run out for all she knew. With no landscape or day or night, it was impossible to calculate time. Jake's wristwatch had stopped, frozen on 11:11 the second they'd entered the cloud. Like Jake, it was motionless.

Coming Halloween 2004

# sean WRight

# Jesse Jameson

## and the Vampire Vault

Book 4

in the highly acclaimed

## Alpha to Omega Series

'Fast becoming a classic series.'

Alison Cresswell, producer of JK Rowling's Omnibus documentary

Published Spring 2005

# sean wright

# Jesse Jameson

## and the Stonehenge of Spelfindial

Book 5

in the highly acclaimed

## Alpha to Omega Series

'Readers and listeners alike were spellbound.'

BBC's Big Read-a-thon (Praise for Book 1 *The Golden Glow*)

Coming Autumn 2005

# sean wright

# Jesse Jameson

## and the Earthwitch of Evenstorm

Book 6

in the highly acclaimed

**Alpha to Omega Series**

'I can see why you have so many fans.'

Caradoc King, Philip Pullman's literary agent

For the latest Jesse Jameson updates visit

www.seanwright.co.uk

Contact the author

sean@seanwright.co.uk

and let him know what you think about

# Jesse Jameson

## and the Curse of Caldazar

THE JOURNEY NEVER ENDS ...